All the Way

Also by Kristen Proby

The Romancing Manhattan Series
All the Way

The Fusion Series
Listen to Me
Close to You
Blush for Me
The Beauty of Us
Savor You

The Boudreaux Series
Easy Love
Easy with You
Easy Charm
Easy Melody
Easy for Keeps
Easy Kisses
Easy Magic
Easy Nights

With Me in Seattle Series
Come Away With Me
Under the Mistletoe With Me
Fight With Me
Play With Me
Rock With Me
Safe With Me
Tied With Me
Breathe With Me
Forever With Me
Stay With Me

Love Under the Big Sky Series
Loving Cara
Seducing Lauren
Falling for Jillian
Saving Grace
Charming Hannah
Kissing Jenna

All the
Way

A Romancing Manhattan Novel

KRISTEN PROBY

wm

WILLIAM MORROW
An Imprint of HarperCollinsPublishers

ALL THE WAY. Copyright © 2018 by Kristen Proby. All rights reserved.
Printed in the United States of America. No part of this book may be
used or reproduced in any manner whatsoever without written permission
except in the case of brief quotations embodied in critical articles and reviews. For information, address HarperCollins Publishers, 195 Broadway,
New York, NY 10007.

HarperCollins books may be purchased for educational, business, or sales
promotional use. For information, please email the Special Markets De-
partment at SPsales@harpercollins.com.

FIRST EDITION

Designed by Diahann Sturge

Library of Congress Cataloging-in-Publication Data has been applied for.

ISBN 978-0-06-267491-3

18 19 20 21 22 LSC 10 9 8 7 6 5 4 3 2 1

This book is for Tessa, my editor. Thank you, for everything.

Acknowledgments

There are always so many people to thank, so many hours put in by the whole team in writing and releasing a new book into the world.

I would like to thank my agent, Kevan Lyon, for being a rock in this sometimes topsy-turvy publishing world. I am so grateful for you!

To Tessa Woodward, my editor at William Morrow, thank you for all of the hard work that you put into every single book. *All the Way*, in particular, was a tricky one, and I appreciate your dedication to making sure this book was everything that it could be.

I need to also thank my team: Pamela Carrion, Lori Francis, Nina Grinstead, and Rachel Starr. Thank you for everything that you do for me, every day.

To my family: thank you for your unwavering love and support.

And to John: You are the best part of every day. Always.

Prologue

~London~

It's about fucking time," my brother, Kyle, snarls from his seat next to me. He's twitchy and mean, both indicative of the drugs coursing through his veins. Although he always had a mean streak. The drugs just make it worse.

"Your sister has been in the hospital and your parents' property had to go through probate," Finn Cavanaugh, my parents' attorney, replies from across the desk. He's a tall man, broad-shouldered in his fancy suit, and his dark hair is short, styled impeccably around his masculine face.

He's much younger than I expected.

"Like I give a shit," Kyle replies, and sends me a sneer. "You're just being a fucking baby."

"Or, you know, I jumped out of a second-story window while my parents burned to death and broke my leg in four places." I shrug and then shake my head and dig my fingertips into my forehead, praying for the incessant pounding there to ease. "I lost everything."

"Drama queen." Kyle rolls his eyes and rubs his dirty fingers over his mouth.

"I can't work," I remind him.

"You're rich."

Same argument, different venue. "I can't dance with this leg, which means I can't work."

"Poor baby," he says, and then lets out a manic laugh. "Who cares? You're getting too fucking old for Broadway anyway. They were about to can your ass. I hope you saved some of that money they've been paying you."

More bullets to my ego, my heart. My head. Because he's not exactly wrong. Thirty-two is old for show business.

But damn it, I love it. And I wanted to leave under my own terms. Not because my parents were killed and I was hurt in the process.

"Let's get to this, shall we?" Finn asks, and slides a bottle of water my way.

"Yeah, let's do it. How much do I get?" Kyle asks, and waits, his eyes pinned on Finn. His foot is bouncing, making that *thump thump thump* noise with each motion, and I want to beat him over the head with my crutch.

"I can read this in its entirety, or—"

"Just get to the fucking chase. What do I get?"

Finn sighs and glances to me, shuts the folder in front of him, and folds his hands on his desk.

"Kyle, your parents set up a trust for you. You will receive fifteen hundred dollars per month to cover your rent and utilities, with the stipulation that you enter drug rehabilitation and finish the program. After one year of sobriety, and with regular clean blood tests, the trust will award you a lump sum of fifty thousand dollars each year until your death."

"What?"

I glance at Kyle and see that his face has gone bright red with fury.

"If you refuse treatment, you forfeit any and all inheritance."

Kyle's mouth bobs open and closed for several seconds, and then he turns to me, royally pissed off.

"Did you do this?"

"Like I had any idea what Mom and Dad put in their will." I roll my eyes and grip my hands in fists in my lap while Kyle stands and begins pacing the room. "You may want to call security."

Finn nods and presses a button while he continues to watch Kyle. He looks calm, but his jaw twitches, and I can see that he's angry at Kyle's behavior as well.

"What does she get?" Kyle demands, pointing at my head.

"Everything else," Finn replies simply. "Your father's partnership in his firm will be sold. London inherits the properties and all of the other monies."

"Are you fucking kidding me?" Kyle roars, leaning over Finn's desk. "She stole my money! That belongs to *me*! She has plenty of her own goddamn money. What am I supposed to do? I have

nothing because those people wouldn't help me, and now I'm left with nothing again?"

"No, you can take the option of getting help," Finn reminds him, but I just shake my head. That's not going to happen. We've been trying to do this for *years*. "The rehab would be paid for, and you can stay there until you feel confident that you're ready to rejoin society."

"Bullshit," Kyle bites out, and sweeps all of Finn's papers off of his desk in one big motion. "I should kick your motherfucking ass."

"Enough!" I yell just as three security guards come inside and take him by the arms to escort him out.

"This is bullshit," he repeats as he's dragged down the hallway. The door closes behind them, but I can still hear him yelling.

Finn and I sit in silence for a long moment. I wish my leg wasn't broken because I'd love to stand and walk to the windows that look out over Manhattan. Mostly, I'd like to turn away from Finn so he can't see the absolute anguish on my face.

I'm an actress. A Tony Award–winning one, at that, but I just can't hide my feelings today.

"I'm sorry," I say at last, and clear my throat. "As you can see, my brother isn't well."

Finn doesn't say anything, he just reaches for his phone and calls his assistant. "Please bring in some hot tea."

He hangs up and watches me in silence until the tea arrives. He pours us each a cup and passes one to me, along with sweetener and milk, and when we both have our tea the way we like it, he says, "Do I have to worry about him coming after you to hurt you?"

I glance up in surprise. "He doesn't know where I live."

He pins me with those chocolate-brown eyes. "Do you honestly believe that?"

I take a sip of my Earl Grey and then sigh. "No. I'm sure he could find me. My building is secure. I'm not worried about him."

"I can file a restraining order."

I laugh. "For what? A piece of paper isn't going to stop him if he gets it in his head to find and hurt me." I shake my head and take another sip of tea. "No, I've dealt with him and his issues most of my life. He'll disappear for a while now, do God knows what, until he runs out of money again and calls me."

"Do you give him money?"

"Not anymore." I squirm in my seat and then set my tea aside. "Thanks for the tea, but I'm okay. We can finish this."

Finn opens the folders and passes me forms to sign, explaining how the properties will be transferred to my name.

"You're a very wealthy woman, London."

"I was wealthy before this," I reply, hearing the hollowness in my voice. "I didn't need my parents to die in order to have money."

"Of course not," he says, shaking his head. "I meant no disrespect."

My leg is beginning to ache again. I've only been taking the bare minimum of the pain meds, unwilling to be in a constant hazy coma. But damn, it hurts today.

"If we're finished, I'll go."

"Can I give you a ride home?" he asks, standing with me. I reach for my crutches and get myself situated.

"I have a car and driver."

He nods and shoves his hands in his pockets. "Can I take you to dinner?"

I glance up in surprise. Finn's a sexy man, and under normal circumstances, I'd do more than let him buy me dinner.

But these aren't normal circumstances.

"Seriously?" I tip my head to the side and scowl at him, no longer surprised, and fully irritated. "You're asking me out just after you've read my parents' will?"

He rubs his fingers over his mouth and then shakes his head, as if he's at a loss for words, and escorts me out to the elevator. "Just call if you have any questions or need anything at all."

"I have one question. Now that I own all of the properties, can I live in them?"

"Of course."

I step into the elevator, turn to face him, and offer him a small smile. "Thanks."

Chapter One

~London~

*T*hree months a year. That's how much time I spent here on Martha's Vineyard off the coast of Massachusetts each summer of my entire life. The rest of the year we lived in Connecticut, so my brother and I could go to school and do what families do.

But every summer, from the day after school let out until the day before we went back, my family lived here, on the beach in the West Chop area of the island. Our house is massive, and worth several million dollars, but as a child, I didn't know that. I just knew that it was a magical place of sunshine and water, of summertime friends that came back every year. Of daydreams and happiness.

It was more home to me than our "full-time" house then, and it still is.

So when Finn told me two months ago that I had inherited all of my parents' properties, and that I could live in them or do what I wished with them, I knew that I'd come here for the summer.

Home.

I'm walking on the beach, without a cane now, thank you very much, enjoying the breeze from the ocean. I have over a hundred feet of private beach, but I can hear kids playing off in the distance, and sailboats are gently meandering by with bright sails and happy people.

At least, they're happy in my head.

Walking in the sand isn't as easy as I would like. My leg aches like a toothache, but it's healing. Slower than I'd like, but it's getting there.

The sand is warm beneath my bare feet, and I have to hold my dark hair off of my face as I stop and look out at the choppy water.

"Because I just have to be meeeee . . ."

I glance over my shoulder at the sound of the small voice and smile. A little girl with a riot of dark curls is dancing down the beach, making grand gestures with her arms and singing loudly. Ironically, she's singing the song from the musical that I starred in for over a year on Broadway.

She stops when she sees me and glances around like she's not quite sure how she got here.

"You have a pretty voice," I say kindly.

"Thanks," she says, and shrugs one shoulder. She's tall, but I don't know kids well enough to know if she's tall for her age. Her eyes are sky blue, standing out against her olive skin and dark hair. "It's my favorite musical."

I nod, smiling. "Mine too."

"Is that your house?" she asks, pointing behind me.

"It is," I confirm. "Where do you live?"

"Over there," she says with a sigh, pointing to the house next to mine. "But ours doesn't have a pool or a playhouse like yours."

I tilt my head to the side, watching her. "You must have had a look around, since I don't think you can see all of that from your house."

She shrugs one shoulder again. "Yeah. I guess."

"Gabby!" A man comes running down the beach, a scowl on his face. "You know this isn't our beach. You can't just run off like that."

Gabby rolls her eyes and then turns back to him, and as he gets closer, I immediately recognize him.

Finn Cavanaugh.

"I'm right here," she says.

"Hey," he says to me, and offers me a small smile. "Sorry if she was bothering you."

Gabby rolls her eyes again, and I can't help but laugh a little. "She's not bothering me at all. We were talking about musicals."

His lips twitch, and I'm reminded just how handsome Finn is. Scratch that. Not handsome.

Fucking hot.

Just my luck, he's my neighbor.

Which I knew, I just forgot.

"How are you feeling?" he asks as Gabby twirls in a circle and dances away to sing and dance some more.

"Better," I reply. "Not fantastic, but I'm finally rid of the crutches and cane, so I'll take it."

"You look good," he says, and then clears his throat. "Any issues?"

Oh, you know, my parents are dead and have left me with a mess to clean up all by myself, my leg is killing me, and I'm pretty sure I lost my career, but nothing major.

"No, I'm good."

He watches me for a moment and then nods. His hands are in his pockets the same way they were in his office two months ago, but this time he's not wearing a suit. No, he's in a red T-shirt and black cargo shorts with no shoes.

I had no idea the casual look could be sexier than the suit, but here we are.

"Your daughter is beautiful."

He grins and glances at Gabby, then turns back to me. "She's my niece. She's staying with me for about a month."

"Oh, that's nice."

He frowns and looks down, and I feel like I've said the wrong thing, but the moment passes and he calls over to Gabby, "It's about time for your horse-riding lesson, Gabs. We should go."

"Fine," she replies with a heavy sigh, and takes off running toward his house.

"She doesn't like horses?" I ask.

"She does, she's just been difficult lately, so very little makes her particularly happy. It's a long story."

"Well, I don't want to keep you." I step back and offer him a smile. "Oh, before you go, it finally clicks as to why you represented my parents. You're the neighbor."

"I've spent the past five summers here," he confirms. "I liked your parents very much. Your dad asked me to update his will about two years ago."

I nod. "Makes sense. Have a good day."

"You too, London."

And with that, he turns and jogs down the beach back to his own house, which is only about a hundred yards from mine. His shoulders are ridiculously broad, especially from behind.

And speaking of behinds, his ass is something to write home about.

Or something to grip on to while he fucks a girl silly.

I clear my throat and shake my head as I walk back toward my house. I must be feeling better if I'm undressing the sexy neighbor with my eyes. I'm not irritated with him anymore for asking me out on that day at his office. That doesn't mean that it wasn't inappropriate. Because it was.

But on a scale of one to house fires on the life-altering scale, that would be a negative fourteen.

I walk up the sandy path to the house, brush my feet clean, and walk inside through the screened sun porch to the kitchen. I brewed some iced tea this morning, so I pour myself a glass, add some lemon, and carry it with me to the library, where I've been working all morning on sorting books.

Mom loved to read. She has to have more than a thousand

books in here, everything from outdated encyclopedias to paperback romance novels. Thrillers, true crime, interior design, and biographies are in there too.

And pretty much everything else.

I remember when we'd come here in the summer, I'd be playing at the beach or in the pool with friends, and Mom would be on the sun porch with a book and a glass of tea, absorbed in another world, but ready for us in case we needed anything.

I sit at her desk and take a sip of my tea before carefully placing it on a coaster and reaching for another stack of books.

Some of them are signed by the authors, so it's not just a matter of donating the ones that I won't read or don't need. I have to look at every single one of them, check for a signature, notes or thoughts that Mom might have written in them, pressed flowers, you name it.

It's become a long process.

I have two boxes nearby. One for donations and one for trash. I mean, who needs an encyclopedia from 1987? Not me. That's what Google is for. And there are plenty of books that are empty and would be welcome at a library or the Goodwill.

Just as I toss a paperback into a box, my phone pings with a text.

What are you doing? It's from Sasha, a former colleague and my best friend. She's in New York, working on a new play that debuts in six weeks, but she texts or calls every single day, checking in on me.

Sorting books in the library. What are you doing?

I set the phone aside, take a sip of my tea, and glance out the window as a huge sailboat with a bright-blue sail soars past.

Having lunch before I head back to rehearsal. Are you ready to sort through your parents' things? They haven't been gone long.

I smile at her concern. She's always been a mother hen.

I can't just sit in this big house and do nothing. I might as well get something accomplished. It's just the library.

Not their bedroom, or the kitchen, where Mom's special dishes are. Those two rooms will have to wait for quite some time.

Don't overdo it. When is your next PT?

Now I feel like Gabby when I roll my eyes and reply.

Tomorrow. Go to rehearsal and stop harassing me.

I grin and rub my thigh where it's started to ache again. I'll take more Advil when I go downstairs.

Fine. You're so difficult. Call you later!

I shove my phone in my pocket, and now that I've gone through that stack of books, I decide to go downstairs rather than reach for more. They're heavy, and I'm tired. One thing I've learned during this whole damn mess is to listen to my body and not push it too hard. If I'm tired, I need to nap. If I hurt, I need to take something. Being miserable isn't worth being stubborn.

I hobble slowly down the stairs to the kitchen and take two Advil, and then wander to my favorite napping spot on the porch. I'll let the ocean breeze lull me to sleep.

I DON'T KNOW what the fuck I'm doing.

I'm standing in my driveway, the hood of my car open, and I'm staring at it as if it just magically holds all of the answers.

So far, all I see is a bunch of stuff that I know absolutely nothing about.

All I do know for sure is, the damn car won't start.

"Don't do this to me today," I plead with the three-year-old BMW. "I have to go to PT today, and I'm already running late. Please start."

With that, I march around to the driver's side, prop my ass on the seat, and push the start button.

Nothing.

"What the hell?"

I get out and face the open engine again, frowning as if it's scorned me on purpose.

"Okay, maybe Siri knows." I pull the app up on my phone

and speak into it. "Siri, my BMW won't start. Can you diagnose the problem?"

"I'm sorry, I don't understand."

I roll my eyes and try again.

"Why won't my BMW start?"

She thinks for a second. "I can't find that answer."

I groan and then try again.

"Siri, please give me possible reasons for why my BMW engine won't start."

"You should seek a professional."

I close my eyes and take a deep breath. "Yeah, no shit. Why are you always such a bitch to me, Siri?"

I hear movement behind me and startle when I see Finn standing there, his hands on his lean hips and a smirk on that sexy face of his.

"How long have you been there?"

"Long enough to hear you have an argument with Siri."

"I thought this was a *smart* phone." I wag it in the air. "If that's the case, wouldn't she know what's going on?"

"In theory. Maybe someday they'll be that smart."

I sigh and turn back to the car. "I guess I'll call AAA."

"Well, hold on. What's wrong?"

"It won't start. It doesn't even make a noise. Just . . . *nothing*."

He steps up beside me and glances inside. Suddenly he reaches in and wiggles something around.

"Try it again."

"Seriously, I can call someone."

"London." He looks down at me with hot brown eyes now and leans both hands on the car, as if he's keeping himself from touching me.

Which is completely all in my head and wishful thinking because he's a stranger and I've been without sex for way too long.

"Yeah?"

"Try it again."

"Okay, I'll humor you, but I really think it's something far more serious than that." I prop my ass on the seat again and push the button, and just like that, the car comes to life. "What did you do?"

"The cable to the battery was loose, which is odd, but not impossible, I guess. It should be fine now."

"Thanks." I check the time and swear under my breath. "I'm late, and they won't see me now. I'll have to reschedule my appointment."

"So you're free for a while?" he asks, and I look up to find him smiling at me.

"Depends."

"Well, how about if I take you to lunch?"

"If you're going to feed me, yes, I'm free." I smile and then blink, remembering that he showed up out of nowhere. "Wait. Why did you come over here?"

"I was walking out to my own car and heard you talking to Siri," he says with a shrug. "I wasn't trying to be nosy, but I figured you could use a hand."

"Thanks."

He nods. "So, lunch?"

"Where's Gabby?"

"I have to pick her up from piano lessons. She'll join us, if that doesn't bother you."

"That doesn't bother me."

"Great." He waits for me to follow him over to his car, opens the door for me, and pulls out of his driveway.

"So, Gabby had horseback-riding lessons yesterday, and piano lessons today?"

"Yes," he says with a nod. "I have her in several activities. I want her to meet other kids and have fun."

"I don't mean to pry, but is she okay?"

He sighs and signals to make a turn. "I'm not sure what's up with her. She's been really challenging for her dad, so I offered to bring her here for a few weeks to give him a break. I was hoping it would help her attitude, but so far it hasn't."

"Where's her mom?"

"She passed away about five years ago," he replies. "Her mom was my younger sister. Carter, Gabby's dad, is still a good friend, and a partner at the firm, and he was about at his wit's end with her."

"Maybe she's just going through a rough patch."

He nods and swings into a driveway where Gabby is waiting on the porch of a house with a grandmotherly woman waiting with her. She waves at Finn as Gabby runs down to the car.

"She's in my seat," she grumbles as she climbs into the backseat.

"London is my guest and you'll be polite, young lady," Finn says, staring her down in the rearview mirror. "Apologize for being rude."

"Sorry," she says, and looks out her window as Finn pulls out of the driveway. He takes us to a restaurant by the water that is known for its fish and chips.

"I love this place," I say when he finds a space to park. "I've come here since I was a kid."

"Perfect," he says with a smile, and we all climb out of the car and get settled at a table inside. Once we've ordered our lunch and have our drinks, I take a sip of lemonade and turn to Gabby.

"So, what musicals are your favorite, Gabby?"

"*A Summer's Evening* is my favorite," she says, not looking me in the eyes.

"Really? That's the musical that I acted in for a few years."

She nods. "Yeah, I know. My dad took me a couple of times."

She shrugs a shoulder, like it's no big deal. Which is fine with me.

"Uncle Finn has me in those stupid piano lessons, but I'd rather learn how to sing better."

I glance up at Finn. "Well, I can give you voice lessons."

Her eyes fly up to mine, holding a little bit of hope now. "You could?"

"Sure." I shrug, as if it's no big deal, mimicking her movement from a few seconds ago, and wink at Finn. "I mean, I've taken voice and dance since I was a little girl. I could totally help you."

She clears her throat and then nods. "Yeah, that could be cool."

"Okay, well, when it works with your schedule, we'll do that."

Our food is delivered, and I dig in, suddenly realizing that I'm starving. The meal is full of fat and oil. Tons of carbs. And I don't even care.

When my basket is empty, I sit back and pat my food belly. "Good lord, that was good. What did you think, Gabby?"

"Pretty good," she admits, and gives Finn the side-eye, not wanting to show too much enthusiasm.

"Thanks for inviting me along. What do you guys have planned for the rest of the day?"

"Gabby has her first karate lesson," Finn says, and my head spins. Good God, she goes nonstop, and it's her summer vacation.

"You're a busy girl."

"Tell me about it," she says, rolling her eyes again. "I thought we would come here to relax, I mean, school's out and all, but Uncle Finn has me doing *everything*."

"I don't want you to be bored," he says, and nudges her with his elbow, but she scoots away from him. She doesn't see the look of hurt in his eyes, and I feel badly for him.

"There are a ton of fun things to do here," I reply. "Have you thought of sailing lessons?"

"I don't like the water," she says, shaking her head.

"Okay. Well, I think karate sounds fun."

She just shrugs again and looks out the window, ignoring us both now.

"What about you?" Finn asks me. "What do you have planned?"

"Well, thanks to my car, I missed my PT appointment, so I'll have to reschedule that. I was going to do some baking this evening."

"What are you making?" Gabby asks.

"Pies. Maybe some cookies. I'll bring you guys some. I love to bake, but I can't eat any of it."

"None of it?" Gabby asks with wide eyes.

"Nope, I have to stay in shape for my job."

I blink rapidly, realizing that I probably *don't* have a job to stay in shape for, but I don't say that. Staying in good physical condition is a habit, and even if I don't get to dance onstage again, it's a healthy habit to have.

"I love pie," Gabby says with a bright smile.

"I thought you might."

Chapter Two

~London~

"Hey gorgeous," my agent, Elizabeth, says into the phone the following day as I'm on my way to PT.

"Hi. Please tell me you have good news."

She sighs, and I park, shove the car out of gear, and prepare myself for the worst.

"I don't think this is what you're going to want to hear," she says. "Roger, the producer of *A Summer's Evening,* has decided to replace you permanently."

My eyes close, my heartbeat speeds up, and I shake my head slowly. "Liz, I'm working my ass off to get better."

"I know that, and so does he, but, honey, you've been gone for almost four months. He has to replace you. You know this."

I nod, not caring in the least that she can't see me. "Okay, so what now?"

"I don't have anything on the line for you right now, London."

"I want to work. I know that everyone thinks that I can't come back from this, and maybe I can't, but I'm *trying*."

"I want you to take the time you need to heal, London. You're respected in this community. And if you can't come back as a dancer, there will still be a place for you here."

I swallow hard, longing to believe her. "Okay."

"Just keep me posted on your progress," she says. We end the call, and I walk into therapy, already feeling both defeated and determined at the same time. Halfway into our session, I blow out a frustrated breath.

"You're doing great," my physical therapist, Joe, says as he stretches my leg out behind me.

"Don't blow smoke up my ass," I reply. "I'm not doing great. It fucking hurts, and my range of motion is for shit. I should be doing better than this, Joe."

"Whoa," he says, and guides my leg down, then turns me to face him. "Talk to me."

"I missed my appointment the other day," I say, as if he should already know all of this. "Which means that I fell back again. And it's been hurting like a mother lately."

"The rain will do it," he replies reasonably. It started raining yesterday afternoon and hasn't let up since. "Are you taking your pain meds?"

"Advil," I reply with a shrug. "I have an addict brother, and the narcotics make me spacey. I don't like it."

"Okay," he says with a nod. "I get it. Have you been using your cane?"

I look down without answering him and he shakes his head.

"London, I need you to use the cane, especially on stairs and on the beach."

"I hate it," I mutter, and then rub my hands over my face in irritation. "I hate all of this. I'm sorry that I'm being a bitch this morning, it just all sucks. And I feel like I'm not making any gains at all."

"You are, I can see them. But you're holding a lot in, and I can see that too. You're angry."

"I can't see the progress." I stare up at him. "And why shouldn't I be angry? I was officially fired today. What if this is as good as it gets, Joe?"

"Well, first of all, it's not. You're still going to improve, you just have to give yourself time. You need to work on healing yourself. Your *whole* self, London, not just the leg. And second of all, there will be other jobs."

I shake my head. "I don't expect you to understand, but every single day that I'm away from New York, the more my career slips out of my fingers. Do you think they'll wait? Because they won't. Of course they feel badly that this happened, but there are a hundred girls behind me who would do more than any of us are comfortable with to get a role. Younger, with more energy, and without an injured leg."

"We're going to get you through this," he promises.

"I should feel better than I do," I insist.

"Your body is different from anyone else's, London. You have a dancer's body, which means that your muscles have been used to being stretched, moved, and exercised every single day for most of your life. For the past four months, you haven't been able to do that, so they've tightened more than an average person's would. You're not just starting from square one, you're even farther behind than that."

"Yay me," I reply, but look him square in the face. "I want to get through this, better than before, and work again."

"Good girl. Now, enough slacking. Let's get this done."

For the next thirty minutes, he puts me through the paces. Exercises with weights, without weights, more stretching. Finally, he has me lie on a table so he can massage the abused muscles.

Believe it or not, that's the part that hurts the most.

I want to cry when he finally lets me get up to leave. I'm sick of hurting.

"You did great today," he says, and laughs when I flip him the bird. "You did. I wouldn't just say that. I'll see you in two days."

I smile and limp out to my car, then just sit in the driver's seat, feeling the steady thump in my leg and listening to the sound of the rain on the roof.

I hope it doesn't turn into a raging storm. I hate those. They terrify me.

I shake my head, start the car, and head toward home. With the weather as bad as it is, traffic isn't too bad. I wouldn't have gone out if I didn't have to either.

The drive home is roughly ten minutes. I pull into the garage and walk inside, not at all excited about walking up the stairs, but I have to.

I still have work to do.

I finished the library this morning and decided that I'd take a stab at Dad's office today. I cave and use my cane to help me get up the stairs. It's a slow, painful process, but once I'm in the office, I forget about the pain and just look around the room.

Where Mom's library was soft and feminine, with pretty upholstered chairs and dainty-looking tables, Dad's office is the exact opposite. The walls are lined with gleaming honey-colored wood. There are shelves covered with heavy, leather-bound books and a large, wide desk that faces the water.

I didn't spend much time in here as a child. The only time I was called in here was if I was in trouble, not unlike being called to the principal's office. This room was designed to be masculine and intimidating, like the man who lived in it, and the designer did a good job of it.

I sit in his big leather chair and let it rock back and forth, running my fingers over the smooth wood of his desk. It still smells like him in here, like peppermint with a hint of tobacco. It brings an unexpected tear to my eye.

I've never considered myself a sentimental person. I don't hold on to much. I'm not a hoarder. So I didn't think it would be so hard to go through my parents' things and try to part with them.

It's kind of like losing them all over again, and I wasn't prepared for that.

Thankfully, this wasn't Dad's full-time office, so I don't have to tackle too much paperwork. And what is here, I can box up and have sent to the house in Greenwich so I can go through all of it at one time later.

I'll have to have someone come help me. I won't know what to save and what to shred.

But no need to think about that right now.

Going through Dad's desk, I find photos and journals, newspaper clippings from the reviews of my work on Broadway, which surprises me. Check that; it shocks the fuck out of me.

I didn't think Dad was particularly sentimental either. Not to mention, a Broadway career was absolutely *not* what he had in mind for his daughter, and he made no secret of his opinion. Seeing the clippings from my shows touches me deeply.

He was proud of me after all.

There's a Valentine's Day card that Mom gave to him. It's dated 1998, and it's super mushy, which makes me grin.

I spend two hours sifting and sorting, and am surprised to realize that not one thing ended up in the trash can. That can't be right. What am I going to do with all of this?

I shake my head and rub my leg, reminded that I worked hard today and I need to take something for it. So I reach for the cane and hobble down to the kitchen. I make myself a cup of coffee, reach for a cookie, and walk out to the porch. I have the outdoor heater on so I can still enjoy the view out here, even with the stormy weather.

"I don't want to!" I hear Gabby yell next door. I don't know why she's outside, but I remind myself that it's none of my business and take a sip of my coffee.

I can barely make out the low murmur of Finn's voice, and then Gabby yells back at him.

"I hate karate! It's dumb! I don't know why you're making me do this. Why can't I take jujitsu? It's better than stupid karate!"

I can't make out Finn's words, but he replies calmly, and then Gabby continues her tirade.

"You're so mean to me! I don't know why you have to be like this. I hate you!"

I cringe. Oh man, stab to the heart.

"Gabby," he says, loudly now, which surprises me. "I'm trying my best here!"

There's no more yelling, and a few minutes later I hear his car start and pull away.

I can't help but remember the brief moment of hurt that passed across Finn's face yesterday afternoon. He loves Gabby very much, it's painfully obvious. He wasn't lying when he said he's trying. I honestly feel badly for both of them.

I hope Gabby comes around sooner rather than later.

Suddenly my phone rings, making me forget all about Finn and Gabby.

"Hi there."

"Hey stranger," Sasha says, chewing something in my ear. "Whatcha doing?"

"I'm sitting on the porch with a cup of coffee," I reply. "Would you like me to start keeping a journal of my comings and goings for you?"

"Yeah, that would be easier," she says, not bothered by my bitchiness in the least. "Just e-mail it to me every evening."

"Smartass." She chews something else. "What are you eating?"

"Celery." She swallows and goes quiet, I'm assuming because she's drinking something. "Dinner of champions."

"Yes, it is. I'm eating a cookie." I take a bite.

"Bitch. I haven't had a cookie in two years."

I laugh, happy to hear from her. "Life's too short to not eat cookies."

"My ass gets too big," she says. "And then my costumes don't fit and the seamstress gets catty about it."

"Easier to not eat the cookies, I guess."

"Yeah, but I do miss them."

"Come visit me and I'll give you all the cookies you want. Also, now is a good time to mention that I can eat all the fucking cookies I want. I'm officially fired."

"Oh, babe," she says, and I can hear the sadness in her voice. "I'm sorry."

"Yeah, well, it was bound to happen, right? I worked my ass off in therapy today, and I've decided that I'll get back to work and prove everyone wrong."

"That's my girl."

"You really should come out here for a few days. It's awesome."

"I'd love to, but I can't get away for a while. Are you coming to opening night?"

"Wild horses couldn't keep me away," I assure her. "How's the weather there?"

"Shitty. It's been raining like crazy."

"Here too." I sigh. "Have you checked on my apartment lately?"

"Yesterday. Everything was fine. I borrowed some shoes too."

I laugh and take another bite of my cookie. "You best return them if you know what's good for you."

"Yes, ma'am. Don't worry, I won't hurt them." She speaks to someone and then returns to me. "I'm sorry, I have to go. We're having an evening rehearsal. I love you, and I'll call you tomorrow."

"Love you too."

She hangs up, and I lean my head back, imagining what she's doing now. Jogging off to her place on the stage, script in hand, ready to get back to work.

I miss it.

More than I thought I would, and that was a lot.

I just fucking miss it.

And I'll be damned if I won't do it again. I worked too hard to reach where I was in my career to let this destroy it.

I MUST HAVE fallen asleep on the porch. It's dark when I wake up to someone ringing the front doorbell.

I stumble through the house, my leg singing in pain, and open the door to find a drenched Finn on the other side.

"Is she here?" he asks right away.

"Gabby? No." I step back and let him in out of the weather. "What's going on?"

"She ran off. Again." He runs his hand through his wet hair. He's breathing hard, his chest rising and falling with each breath. "She's mad at me. Also again."

"She can't have gone far," I reply, and open a closet to reach for a pair of shoes and a flashlight. "I'll help you look."

"I've already run up and down the beach and didn't see her," he says. "London, if she was on the beach in the dark—"

She could be killed.

"I know, but she's not on the beach. She's just hiding because she's mad." I rub his arm soothingly and check the flashlight for batteries, which thankfully seem to work. "Besides, I think I know where she is."

"Lead the way."

We walk through the house to the back door, and I lead him outside to the small replica of the house my father had made for me when I was about Gabby's age.

"I didn't know this was back here," he says.

"Gabby did. She mentioned it to me when I saw her on the beach the other day. A light is on in there."

I hear him swear under his breath as I open the door and step inside and find Gabby lying on the small bed inside, hugging my old floppy-eared bunny.

"Hi, Gabby."

She sits up in surprise. "Am I in trouble?"

"Well—" I begin, but Finn cuts me off.

"Hell yes, you're in trouble. You can't just run off on me like that, and you can't break and enter into someone else's property, Gabby. What in the hell are you thinking?"

"I'm mad and I want to be alone," she shouts back at him. "You don't understand me at all!"

And with that, she dramatically throws the bunny on the bed and runs out, toward Finn's place.

He sighs and rubs his hand down his face. "This is a lot of fun."

"Why don't I go back with you and I'll try to talk to her?"

"You don't have to do that."

But he's looking at me with so much hope I know that I can't do anything else.

"I'm happy to. Sometimes a girl has to talk to another girl."

His lips twitch before he leads me out of the playhouse and toward his home. I have to take it slow, limping a bit behind him. He turns back and sees me struggling, so he just picks me up, as if it's the most natural thing in the world, and carries me.

"Hi there, He-Man."

He laughs. "I don't like watching you struggle."

"It seems to be a part of life these days."

I lean my head on his shoulder as the water falls on us, soaking us both. When we reach his house, he opens the door and sets me inside.

"Where's her bedroom?"

"Top of the stairs," he says, pointing up. I cringe inwardly, but I refuse to let him see me struggle any more. Once at the top of the stairs, I take a deep breath and knock on Gabby's door.

"Go away!"

"Gabby, it's me." I crack the door and peek inside. The room is so pretty, with white furniture and pink frilly linens. "Can I come in?"

"Fine," she says, and sniffles.

I walk in and sit at the edge of her bed as she sits up. I pass her a tissue from her bedside table and wait patiently as she wipes her tears and blows her nose.

"I know you feel grown up, but, Gabby, you can't run away like that. Something horrible could happen to you, and that would devastate everyone who loves you."

"I just didn't want to be here anymore, and the man who usually stays out in the playhouse hasn't been there in a while, so I decided to go chill out there."

I still and feel my heart drop into my stomach.

"What man?"

She frowns. "The man that stays in the playhouse," she repeats. "He's there all the time."

I don't want to freak out in front of her. Actually, I *do* want to freak out, but I take a deep breath to stay calm. I'll handle one thing at a time.

"Why didn't you want to be here anymore?"

She shrugs her slender shoulders and buries her face in her knees.

"I miss my mom," she says quietly.

Oh, sweet girl, so do I. I know that I haven't let myself grieve as much as I need to. There are moments when I think that if I give in to the grief, it'll suck me into the deepest, blackest hole and I'll never climb my way out.

I blink my own tears away and reach out to smooth her dark curls from her damp face.

"I recently lost both of my parents," I say, and swallow hard. "So believe me when I say, I sure miss my mom too."

Her head comes up quickly. "I'm sorry."

"You didn't do anything."

"I'm not very nice sometimes." She sniffs again. "I don't know why I act like that. London?"

"Yes?"

"Can I tell you something?"

"Anything."

She swallows hard. "I started bleeding yesterday, and I don't know what to do. Uncle Finn doesn't have anything here for me, so I've just been throwing my underwear away."

"Oh, my goodness, Gabby." I pull her into my arms and hug her close. "Do you know about your period?"

"Yeah, we had a class about it."

"Do you have questions?"

She shakes her head no, and I don't press her.

"Well, you and I need to go get you some things."

I stand up and hold my hand out for her, which she takes, and she follows me down the stairs, patiently walking next to me when I have to move slowly.

Finn is waiting in the living room and looks genuinely surprised to see Gabby holding my hand.

"Finn, Gabby and I need to run an errand."

He frowns. "What kind of errand?"

"I'll explain later—"

"No—" Gabby begins, but I cut her off.

"I'll explain later, but I need you to trust me right now. Gabby and I need to run out for a few things, but we'll be back in about thirty minutes."

"Okay," he says immediately, and I step to him so I can speak low, out of Gabby's range.

"I'll also need to talk to you about someone apparently living in my playhouse. I don't know if it's true, Gabby mentioned it, but it spooked the hell out of me."

"Jesus." He runs his hand down his face. "I'll call the police."

"No, I can deal with it, but—"

"I'll call the damn police." His jaw is firm, ticking, and I know I'm not going to win this battle.

"Please wait to call them until we get back. This is important."

His eyes narrow. He isn't happy, but he nods once.

"Wait here," I say to Gabby. "I'll go get my car and pick you up in ten minutes."

She smiles and I hurry as fast as I can to my house, gather my bag and keys and lock up, then drive over to pick up the little girl, who jumps right into my car and fastens her seat belt.

I drive us to a nearby drugstore and lead Gabby to the feminine hygiene aisle, where we hem and haw about which products she'd like to try. I end up grabbing two different kinds, along with a heating pad, new underwear for her, and a shitload of chocolate, which makes her happy.

"A girl needs lots of chocolate when it's that time of the month," I inform her. "I don't know why, it just makes you feel better."

"I like that part," she says with a smile, and we pay for our things, then go back to Finn's, where once inside, I take Gabby into the bathroom to show her how to use her new tools.

When we come back to the living room, Gabby hugs me tight and says, "Thank you."

And then, to Finn's absolute shock, she launches herself into his arms and hugs him just as tightly. "I'm sorry, Uncle Finn."

She kisses his cheek and then runs up the stairs to her bedroom, shutting the door behind her.

Finn blinks rapidly and then stares at me. "What just happened?"

"She started her period," I reply, and cringe when he hangs his head in his hand. "She didn't know what to do, or who to talk to. So I just got her all set up with everything she needs, and I think she feels better. But it totally explains the mood swings, and her acting out so badly over the past few days."

"Thank you," he says, and then reaches out for my hand and tugs me gently into his arms for a firm hug. "Thank you so much for doing that for her. It's just my luck that this happened when she's with *me*."

"You'll be fine, just be gentle with her for a day or two."

Dear God, his chest is hard.

And he smells so damn good.

I could stand here like this forever if my leg wasn't screaming at me.

"Let me take you to dinner tomorrow night."

"What about Gabby?"

"She's going on a Girl Scout overnighter," he says with a smile.

"You have to say yes!" Gabby yells from upstairs, clearly eavesdropping and making us both laugh.

"Well, sounds like I have to say yes. So, yes. I'd love that."

"Excellent." His dark eyes are still pinned on mine when he calls up to Gabby. "Go to bed, Gabs. We have some things to do down here."

"Okay, good night."

"Now I call the police," he says, and pulls his phone out of his pocket. "If someone's been squatting in that playhouse, you're not going back over there alone."

"Hi, I'm London Watson, an adult. I can make those decisions for myself."

His eyes narrow again just before he speaks into the phone and explains the situation to dispatch. "Thank you. We'll be waiting."

"Are they coming?"

"On their way," he replies. "You should stay here."

"Hell no, I won't stay here." I stand my ground, my hands on my hips, glaring up at him. It seems Finn has a bit of a control-freak side. "It's *my* house, Finn."

He just shakes his head and leads me outside. Two squad cars pull into my driveway, and we meet them on my front porch.

"I'm London Watson, the homeowner," I announce before Finn can say anything.

"Did you see anyone in your home?" one of the officers asks.

"I didn't, no, but Finn's niece says she saw a man living in the playhouse out back."

The officer frowns and shares a look with his colleague. "So *you* didn't actually see him?"

"No." The officer nods.

"Okay, show us the way."

I lead them around the house in the dark, thankful that I left several lights on inside to illuminate the way. Once we reach the playhouse, I stand back and gesture toward it. "This is it."

"Does it have electricity?"

"Yes, the switch is just inside the door."

They step in and turn on the lights and look around. "Would you know if anything was disturbed?"

"I haven't been in here in years," I reply, following them in. The mattress that Gabby was lying on is bare. The furniture is plastic and old, and things are messy, but that's to be expected with years of neglect. "I should probably go through and clear it out, I just haven't had time."

"So, you don't know if anything is missing, or if anyone has been here?"

I glance around again and hug my arms around my middle. "I don't think it looks any different than it did the last time I saw it."

"Gabby could have said it just to scare you," Finn suggests. "We've been having behavioral issues with her lately."

"Well, if you decide that anything is missing or disturbed, give us a call. Sounds like we're done for tonight."

They hand me a business card and then leave, and I'm left standing in my playhouse with Finn.

"It's so odd." I shake my head and look around. "It doesn't look any different. But I don't think Gabby was telling stories."

"It's been her thing lately," Finn says, and pushes my hair over my shoulder. "I'm sorry that she scared you."

"I'm just glad that it's a false alarm."

"Do you want me to stay?"

I smile and shake my head, ready to get off my aching leg. "I'm okay."

"Okay, then, I'll pick you up at seven," he says, and steps forward to wrap me into a hug once again.

A girl could get used to this.

"Oh, quick question. Is this going to be a fancy dinner? Because I'm afraid I didn't bring any fancy clothes with me from New York."

His lips twitch in that way they do when he finds something amusing. Or, you know, when he finds *me* amusing.

"No, casual is great."

"Okay, sounds like a plan. I'll see you at seven."

He nods and waits for me to open the back door before he starts the walk back to his house.

"See you soon, London."

Chapter Three

~Finn~

"Hey Mom," I say into the phone, and frown at Gabby when she tries to sneak another chocolate bar from the cabinet I shoved them into this morning.

She's been stuffing chocolate in her mouth since last night, insisting that it's her *period medicine*.

"What are you doing, dear?" Mom asks.

"I'm trying to keep Gabby from going into a sugar coma," I reply, and shake my head at my niece, who just rolls her eyes and then drops her head in her hand dramatically. "How are you? How is Italy?"

"Oh, I'm just fine. Italy is always glorious, but I'm about to get on a plane home."

"Why? You're not supposed to come home for another month."

"Because I miss my family. I'm coming to your house on Martha's Vineyard for a few days."

I stand up straight and frown, staring unseeingly at the ocean.

"Is that a problem?" she asks when I don't reply right away.

"No, of course not. You know you're always welcome. I have plenty of space."

"I'd like to see Gabby," she says. "I won't stay long."

"It's never an inconvenience to have you here, Mom. When shall I pick you up from the airport?"

Mom rattles off the time. I hang up after wishing her safe travels to find Gabby taking a bite of a Snickers.

"Damn it, Gabby."

She just offers me a big smile and chews happily.

"Since you're not feeling well enough to go overnight tonight, I'm going to cancel my date with London."

"No!" She jumps off her stool and hurries over to me, and takes my hand in hers. "Uncle Finn, you *have* to go. You just *have* to."

"Why?"

"Because you like her, and she's *so* nice, and pretty, and you just have to go. You don't have to worry about me, I can totally stay home by myself. I've done it before."

"I don't think so." I shake my head, but Gabby holds on to my hand even more tightly.

"I'll be totally fine here. You already ordered me a pizza for dinner, and I'm just going to watch a movie on Netflix with my heating pad. Seriously, you can totally trust me."

This little girl says *totally* more than anyone I've ever met in my life.

"I can't chance you running off again, Gabby. I love you more than anything, but you haven't given me much reason to trust you lately. Not to mention scaring London last night with that story about someone staying in her playhouse. That was uncalled for."

She starts to interrupt me, but I hold my hand up and she closes her mouth.

"You can't just scare people like that. It's not funny."

"I'm sorry," she says, and bites her lip. Her blue eyes are big, reminding me of her mom's eyes, and I feel myself soften.

"If I give you back your cell phone—"

"Oh my gosh, *yes!*"

"Which still does not have any data available to you and you can only call me, your dad, or Grandma, who is currently on an airplane, so you can call me if something were to happen."

"*Nothing* is going to happen. I've totally got this."

"We are going to the Lobster Shack," I inform her, and write it down on the pad by the refrigerator. "I'm picking London up at seven, and I'll be home by nine, which is before dark."

"Well, that's a boring date," she says with a laugh.

"Don't push me, Gabby. I shouldn't leave you here in the first place."

But the idea of not seeing London tonight makes me nuts.

Not that I would put Gabby at risk if I thought she couldn't spend two hours by herself. She can, but she's been so . . . *challenging* lately.

"You *should* leave me here. I have food, entertainment, and a way to reach you should there be an emergency." She's put her serious face on now, reminding me of the sweet girl that she's always been.

Reminding me so much of her mother.

It's so damn good to see her again.

"You're funny, you know that?"

"Oh, I'm *totally* funny," she agrees. "And you are going to be late if you don't go."

"I'm early. She lives right next door."

She shrugs and takes a few slices of pizza on a plate into the TV room. "Girls don't like it when a guy is late."

"How do you know this?"

"I've seen movies," she says. "Go have fun. I'm totally fine."

"Yes, so you've said. Here's your phone." I hand it to her and watch as she turns it on with glee. She's been grounded from using it for two months, only getting possession of it when she's at a lesson or somewhere that she may need to reach someone. No chitchat with her friends.

"Can I text Larissa?" she asks.

"Who's Larissa?"

"My best friend," she says. "I haven't talked to her in *forever*."

"Or, you know, since school got out a couple of weeks ago."

"*Forever.*"

"Yes, you can text her, and only her, unless you need to call me or your dad."

She nods happily. I hope I don't live to regret this.

I quickly change into jeans and a black button-down, check my hair, and then run downstairs to say good-bye to Gabby, who barely acknowledges me as she eats her pizza and texts with her friend.

She's going to be okay.

I get in my car and make the quick trip over to London's house, ring her bell, and wait for the gut punch that always happens whenever I see her.

She swings the door open, and sure enough.

Gut punch.

Fucking hell, she's beautiful. Her dark hair is pulled back in a single braid and her blue eyes are wide, her cheeks a bit flushed. She's in a simple blue sundress that manages to make her look even more petite than I remember her being yesterday.

Her legs are bare, and I can't help but imagine what they'd feel like wrapped around my waist while she moans in my ear.

Settle down, Cavanaugh.

"Hey," she says with a smile. "You're a tiny bit early."

"Gabby says girls like that."

She laughs and walks away from me into the house toward the kitchen. She has a slight limp, but it's getting better. I've hated watching her limp. Not because I'm an asshole, but because there's literally *nothing* I can do to help her, and that's just about the worst feeling in the world.

But it's good to see how much progress she's made in her recovery. She's an incredibly strong woman.

"I just have to lock up back here and grab my bag," she says, her back to me. "Is Gabby at her sleepover?"

"No, she insisted that she's not feeling well enough for it, so I told her she could stay home."

"Oh." She stops cold. "She can join us."

I smile at her kindness and cross to her, pulling her into my arms the way I did last night when she'd been so nice to Gabby. She's so fucking small, but she fits against me perfectly. "No," I whisper, and kiss her forehead. "She can't. I love her, but it's time I got some time alone with you."

She takes a deep breath and fists her hands in my shirt at my sides, making me wish I could strip us both naked, boost her on this kitchen counter, and have my way with her.

But we're not there quite yet.

"Does the Lobster Shack sound okay for dinner?" I ask, pulling away and breaking the sexual chemistry.

"Sounds delicious," she says with a smile. "Let's go."

I lead her out, wait for her to lock her door and set the alarm, and then we're on our way to the nearby restaurant.

"So does this mean that Gabby is alone?" she asks.

"It does." My hands tighten on the steering wheel. I'm still not convinced this is a good idea.

"She'll be fine," London says with a confident nod, as if she's trying to convince both of us. "You look nice."

I smile over at her and let my eyes travel leisurely over her body. "You're fucking stunning."

Her eyes widen before I look back at the road and I hear her clear her throat. That's right, the attraction is there.

"Thank you," she says quietly as I park in front of the restaurant. It's on the beach, and serves seafood, as the name suggests. The decor is fishing nets and life preservers, boat oars, stuffed fish. It's as casual as you can get.

We're shown to a table, and the hostess gives us each a plastic bib along with our menus.

"This is sexy," London says when we're alone. "I should wear this daily."

"You'd look amazing in anything," I reply as I tie my bib around my neck. "I wonder how this would look in a court-room."

She snorts out a laugh and covers her mouth with her hand. "I think you should try it. It could be a new fashion sensation."

We order the famous bucket of food and a beer and I check my phone for the fourth time since we got here eight minutes ago.

"She's fine," London says patiently. "I promise."

"If she runs off—"

"She won't." She reaches across the table to take my hand in hers and squeezes tightly. "She's not stupid. Stubborn and moody, but not stupid. She ran away because she knew you'd find her. And now she wants you to trust her."

"You're an intelligent woman," I reply, and guide her hand to my mouth. I plant a kiss on her knuckles before she pulls it away and rests her chin in her hands, watching me.

"I was once a girl her age," she says with a shrug. "Just wait until she's sixteen."

I cringe. "Her dad can handle that."

"You're still close with her dad?" London asks as she takes a sip of her beer.

"Very. He's a partner at our firm. It's me; Gabby's dad, Carter; and my brother, Quinn."

"All three of you are lawyers?"

"Yes."

"Do you handle a lot of estate law?"

I smile and shake my head no. "I did that for your dad because I admired and liked him. I'm a corporate attorney."

"Ah," she says with a nod. "So was Dad. No wonder you got along well. You're awfully young to own a firm, aren't you?"

"How old do you think I am?"

She cocks a brow, and then laughs. "I don't know, thirty-five?"

"I'm almost forty." I take a sip of my beer, waiting for her response, but there isn't one. "Does the age difference bother you?"

"It's eight years," she replies. "I'm not a minor. I think we're good."

I tilt my head to the side, watching her.

"So tell me more," she says. "How did you come to own a successful corporate law firm with your brothers before you're forty?"

"It *is* unusual," I concede. "About five years ago I was an associate attorney at a firm and got the case of my career. I won't bore you with all of the legal terms, but needless to say it made me a lot of money. More than I thought I'd make in my career. So I left that firm and asked my brothers to join me in our own. We've managed to build a reputation and an impressive caseload."

"Your offices are beautiful," she says as the food is delivered. Rather than setting plates in front of us, they dump the food on the table, pass us a mallet, a knife, and a fork, and leave us to our own devices.

"I wonder if they have a bib dress," she says with a smile. "I think this is going to get messy."

"Messy food tastes the best," I reply, and reach for a crab leg, which I smash with the mallet, and immediately spatter us both. "But a bib dress might be a good idea."

She's laughing as she reaches for a small piece of corn on the cob and takes a bite. She squirts juice from the corn across the table and it hits me in the face.

"Who knew dinner would turn into a battlefield?" I ask, laughing so hard my stomach muscles start to hurt.

"Oh my God, I'm sorry," she says, also laughing. She reaches across with her napkin and wipes the juice away. "I'm going to need a shower after this."

And, just like that, my cock is at full attention.

"How did you get into theater?" I ask, ignoring my dick and willing it to calm the fuck down.

"I don't even remember," she says, hammering the hell out of a crab leg. "I've always taken dance and music lessons. I'm quite sure my mom put me in them when I was a toddler. I was like a fish in water." She takes a bite and then gets serious about destroying another leg. "I've never had stage fright. In fact, it's a rush for me. It's like—" She stops to think about it and then shrugs her slender shoulder. "I don't know what it's like. Really good sex, maybe? That euphoric feeling that rushes through you. But rather than just a few seconds, it lasts for a couple of hours when I'm onstage."

"It's adrenaline," I reply, and she nods enthusiastically.

"Yes, absolutely. My mom loved it. She enjoyed the frilly, girly outfits that I'd wear for recitals, and she enjoyed helping my high school with costumes. I think that my mom would have been an amazing fashion designer.

"And my dad was way more reserved."

"Is that code for he hated it?"

"With a passion," she replies with a nod. "He was a controlling man. And he was wealthy, but that money came with strings. His thinking was, if I'm paying for college, or anything else, for that matter, you'll do as I say. But I didn't want to be a doctor, or a lawyer. I wanted to be a performer."

"So how did you manage to talk him into it?"

"We agreed on a school in New York, and I went to school while also auditioning, taking dance and voice classes, and working full-time. I decided that I'd do both, and I'd prove to him that I'd make the performing a success."

I can't take my eyes off of her. Her animation in the way she moves her hands and face while she talks is hypnotizing. It's no wonder she's so successful as a performer.

"Wow, that's a lot of work for a student."

"I didn't care," she replies before taking a bite of a potato. "I wasn't interested in anything else. I was a virgin until I was twenty-two because I didn't give two shits about boys or anything else aside from the work. I graduated with honors and still managed to land roles on Broadway."

"That's amazing," I say. "I'm sure your parents were very proud of you."

"Mom was ecstatic. Dad was reluctantly tolerant."

"That sounds harsh."

She shrugs. "I know. I loved him, very much, but he didn't make it easy for me to be an adult. He liked to have his thumb on all of us. It's why my brother rebelled so strongly. My mom . . . she loved him. And she didn't mind working as a housewife and mother, despite the fact that she could have done so much more."

"She was fulfilled," I suggest.

"I think so." She thinks about it for a moment. "I hope so." She leans back, patting her flat stomach. "I'm full. You're going to have to roll me out of here. My apologies."

I laugh and toss my napkin on the table. "I call uncle too. Are there some of those wet naps over there?"

She searches at the end of the table and comes up with several small packages of the premoistened towelettes so we can wipe our hands mostly clean. Before we take our bibs off, I reach for my phone.

"Do you mind if I take a selfie of us like this?"

"A first-date bib selfie? Doesn't everyone do that?" She leans in to smile for the photo and then we ditch the bibs and I pay the bill.

"I'd like to pick up dessert on our way back," I say as I lead her to the car. "I know it feels like I'm trying to cut this short, and I'm definitely not doing that. I'm having a great time."

"But Gabby is home alone," she says with a nod. "I get it. I've had fun too."

"Why don't we pick something up for all three of us, and we can eat it out on my deck and watch the water?" I suggest, earning a wide smile from her.

"I'd like that. I know a place with great pie."

"Lead the way, my lady."

She directs me to a little shop that you'd miss if you didn't already know it was there. When we step inside, the smell of delicious pie greets us.

"What do you suggest?" I ask London.

"The cran-apple is my favorite," she says. "But really, you can't go wrong with any of it."

"We'll take a cran-apple," I say to the lady behind the sales counter. "Do you sell ice cream here as well?"

"We do," she says with a smile. "Would you like a half gallon of the vanilla?"

"That's perfect."

Before long we're headed home with our treats. Gabby's where I left her less than two hours ago, and barely glances up from her movie when we walk past her to the kitchen.

"So glad we're not burglars," I call out to Gabby, who just waves at me.

"Told you she was okay," London says with a smile, and sits on the stool at the island while I find a knife and plates. I dish us all up, deliver Gabby's to her, and then lead London out to the back deck, which has killer views of the water.

"This is beautiful," London says as she sits with her dessert.

"It's the same view as yours," I remind her.

"Yeah, and it's still beautiful." She smiles and takes a bite of her pie, then lets her head fall back as she moans in happiness. "Oh my God, so good."

"Do you make that noise often when you eat?"

"What noise?"

"The moan."

She frowns. "I don't know, why?"

"Because if you do, I'll have to make sure I don't eat with you anymore. It makes me want to fuck you, London."

She stops, her fork halfway to her mouth, and stares at me with her jaw dropped.

"Well, you're blunt."

"Frankly, I don't know any other way to be right now because I'm so turned on I can barely see straight."

"And flattering."

"I'm not flattering you, I'm being honest." I continue eating my pie, letting the conversation die, and she digs into hers as well. She sets her plate aside when she's finished and, to my surprise, sets mine aside as well before climbing into my lap and wrapping her arms around my neck, threading her fingers in the hair at the back of my head.

"Gabby can't see us," she says quietly.

"No, and she's preoccupied with her movie anyway, but I'm not getting naked with you out here."

She smiles and drags her fingertips down my cheek.

"No, no getting naked tonight. But I've wanted to do this for a few days." She leans in and presses her lips to mine, and I take over, gripping her wrists in my hands and wrapping them behind her back, pressing her chest to mine as my mouth devours her. She's sweeter than the pie, and feels like heaven pressed against me.

She makes that little moan, grinds herself against my cock, which is pressed painfully against my jeans, and I want nothing more than to lay her back, strip her bare, and take my time exploring every fucking inch of her.

But Gabby's here, and we're outside, so this is not the place or the time.

God damn it.

"London," I whisper against her mouth. "As much as I hate myself for it, I have to stop this."

"I know," she says, her eyes closed as she leans her forehead against mine. "What is it about you, Finn Cavanaugh?"

I kiss her nose, her forehead, then let her arms go and she braces herself against my chest as she leans back and stares down at me.

"Don't answer that," she says as she shimmies off of my lap. I see the cringe on her face when she moves her leg a certain way and I feel like a complete douche for not being more careful with her. "I'm not fragile," she says, as if she can read my mind.

"No, you're not."

She clears her throat, brushes some stray hair off her cheek, and seems to wrap her dignity around her.

"You *are* sexy as hell, and I hope I get the chance to see you again," I say as I glide my finger down her bare arm. She sends me a bright, happy smile.

"I'd like to see you again too."

"My mother is arriving in the morning," I reply, and she looks surprised. "She called me today, so it's a last-minute visit, but she'll just be here for a couple days."

"That'll be nice for you and Gabby," London says with a nod.

"Here." I unlock my phone and pass it to her. "Put your number in here so I can call you the minute she leaves."

She smiles again and does as I ask.

"I should go," she says. "If I don't, I'll throw myself at you again, and I limit that to once a day."

"I'll remember that," I reply with a laugh, and stand with her. Rather than walk through the house, she takes the stairs off my deck.

"There's a shortcut to my place down here," she says with a wink. "Just in case you ever need it."

And with that, she's gone, and I'm left sexually frustrated and counting down to when I can see her again.

Two days. I haven't seen London in two days, and it's making me twitchy.

So while my mom and Gabby make breakfast and fuss at each other, I decide to go for a run down the beach. I prefer to go much earlier in the morning when there are fewer people out, but this will do.

I run for about three miles, and then turn around to head back home. When I can see London's house, I slow down. I wonder what she's doing right now, and call myself a fool for not at least texting her over the past couple of days. She probably thinks I'm a jerk.

As I get closer, I see the woman herself standing in the sand, just at the edge of the water. She's in shorts and a tank top with a hoodie wrapped around her waist.

Her dark hair is down, getting blown in the wind.

She's so damn beautiful she takes my breath away.

She turns and sees me and offers me a smile while letting her eyes wander up and down my body. She bites her lip, and I can see the heat in her eyes.

Yes, the attraction is absolutely there.

"Good morning."

"Hi," she says. "How was your run?"

"Good, actually." I stop and prop my hands on my hips, breathing hard. "How are you?"

"Not half bad." She brushes her hair off of her face. "Have you had breakfast?"

"Nope."

"I was just about to make some. Would you like to join me?"

"Yep." I smile and lean in to press a quick kiss to her lips. "Let me run home real quick to clean up and I'll be right over."

"Sounds great. See you in a few."

I kiss her once again, then jog into the house and open the fridge for a bottle of water.

"I hope you're hungry," Mom says. "I've made waffles for all of us."

"I'm eating breakfast with London today," I inform her, and smile when Gabby claps her hands in happiness.

"Is this the neighbor girl?" Mom asks.

"I don't know any other Londons," I reply, and kiss her cheek. "Sorry to bail on you."

"Oh, please, we're just fine here without you, aren't we, darling girl?"

"We're totally fine," Gabby agrees, and gives me a thumbs-up.

My ten-year-old niece approves of London.

Now I just have to call my brothers and explain why I'm extending my vacation and bailing on work for a few more weeks.

Chapter Four

~London~

*H*e presses his lips to mine quickly, smiles, and jogs off toward his house and I can only stand where I am, my fingers pressed to my lips, and watch his ass as he leaves.

If I didn't know better, I'd say I had a crush on the sexy Finn Cavanaugh.

Strike that. I *do* have a crush on Finn. What's not to like? He's kind, funny, loves his family, and looks like *that*.

So I'm going to spend as much time as I can with him, since he's been the best thing to come into my life since the fire, since the day in his office with my brother, since trying to heal from it all.

He brings a smile to my face and makes me want to climb him like a damn tree, and that's a good feeling.

I take a deep breath and, with a smile, walk into the house to get breakfast started. I had planned to just have a bagel and some egg whites, but now that's changed up a bit. I love to cook, especially for others, so I pull my hair up in a messy bun and stand in the middle of my white kitchen, getting my wits about me.

I could make omelets, or pancakes, or biscuits and gravy.

I buy way too many groceries.

I smirk at myself and decide on biscuits and gravy with home fries and scrambled eggs. It's a heavy breakfast, but it's also delicious, and I want to feed him something especially delicious.

"Like me," I mutter, and then laugh. Oh, the dreams I've been having about Finn the past few nights have been one hundred percent pornographic. I wake up hot and bothered, and not just a little sexually frustrated.

Damn him.

I jump at the soft knock on the back glass door, and turn to find Finn standing there in another pair of cargo shorts and a T-shirt, his hair wet from a shower, grinning at me through the glass.

Hot damn.

I motion for him to come in, and stir the biscuit batter.

"I hope you worked up an appetite on that run," I begin as he walks toward me. "I'm making a feast."

"I'm hungry," he says in a gruff voice, making me glance up at him. He's staring at me with hot eyes. Not just hot. Scorching. Like he wants to do me on the kitchen counter.

I'm not against that in the least.

"Hungry for biscuits and gravy?" I swallow hard.

"We can start there," he says. "You're making it from scratch?"

"Of course." I set the batter aside and gather more supplies. "Isn't that how everyone does it?"

"No, I buy those biscuits in the roll that always scares the shit out of me when I bust it open."

I chuckle as I roll the dough out and cut it into circles. "Well, no scaring the shit out of you today. These don't take long."

"Do you need any help?"

"Nope." I pop the pan in the oven and get started on cutting potatoes. "Actually, yes. How are you at cutting potatoes?"

"I'm a champion potato chopper," he informs me, and takes the knife from me. "I've got this."

"Do you like to cook?" I try to keep my eyes off of his strong hands and muscly forearms as he chops up the potatoes. Why is it that everything he does is sexy?

It's not exactly fair.

"I do," he replies. "I just don't always have time for it."

"I don't either, but it seems I have nothing *but* time lately." I shrug and throw the potatoes in a pan so they can start frying while I get the gravy going. "I've been cooking way more than I can eat."

"How are you feeling?" he asks casually.

"Better," I reply, happy to be able to finally say that truthfully. "I still have moments when it hurts, but I think the walking is better, and my range of motion is coming back. My physical therapist is happy with the progress, but I think it's too slow."

"You're too hard on yourself," he says, and I just shake my head.

"That's what he says too. Being physical is what I've always done. Dance, theater, is physically demanding, and I've always been in excellent shape. So having lost so much of my endurance is disappointing."

"You'll get it back," he says with confidence, and I look up to find him smiling at me, his brown eyes happy. "You're too stubborn to do otherwise."

"Boy, that's the truth." I pull the biscuits out of the oven. "I know that I probably won't be able to work the way I used to. They've already recast my old part, which, let me tell you, will tear your heart right out of your chest."

"I can't even imagine."

"And I'm not young, Finn." I'm just talking now, talking about my career, my fears, and it feels like the easiest thing to do with him. I haven't confided like this with *anyone*. Not even Sasha.

"You're only thirty-two."

"That's old for theater. Especially in musicals. There are girls more than ten years younger than me fighting for the same parts, and they're in better shape, and it's easier for them to keep up with the rigorous schedule."

"Have you seen Hugh Jackman in the musical movies he makes?" Finn asks. "That guy's almost fifty."

"He's a man," I reply simply. "Men are given better roles, longer into their lives. It sucks, but it's true. But I've changed my attitude a bit. I was convinced before that I wouldn't be able to get back to work, but now I'm determined to do exactly that."

"Would you consider doing film? I don't know anything about show business, but I would think that might be less rigorous."

"I hadn't before." I stop and lean my hip against the countertop, irritated that my leg is starting to ache from being on it too long. "But I could talk to my agent and see what she thinks. She's come to me before with scripts, but I have always had a steady job in New York."

"Might be something to consider," he says casually. "You're hurting right now."

"Not too badly."

"Look at me." He grips my shoulders and makes me look him in the eyes. "You're hurting."

"Yeah, it's aching."

"Sit." He leads me to the stool on the other side of the island. "I've got this handled."

"*I'm* supposed to be making *you* breakfast," I reply, and rub my thigh, frustrated with it, but intrigued by the man currently commanding my kitchen. He looks good here.

Really, really good.

"You did," he says. "I'm just finishing up. See, I give this a little stir, and flip the potatoes, and we're good to go."

"You're a nice guy."

He turns and gives me a shocked glare. "Take that back."

"Nope. It's the truth."

"I object."

"This isn't a courtroom," I remind him with a laugh. "You may be tough in a takeover or a merger, or whatever the hell it is that you do, but at the end of the day, you're just a nice guy in a sexy suit."

He cocks a brow. "You think I'm sexy?"

"I think your suit is sexy. That's what I said."

He wanders slowly around the island to stand next to me, and before I know it, he's lifted me onto the countertop and is standing between my legs, his hands flat on the granite at my hips and his face level with mine.

"So you *don't* think I'm sexy?"

Oh, you have no idea.

"I didn't say that either."

His eyes drop to my lips and back up to my eyes. "Is this hurting your leg?"

"I give zero fucks about my leg right now."

"That's not what I asked."

I tilt my head to the side. "No. It doesn't hurt it."

Any more than it already hurt.

"Let me tell you this," he says gruffly. "I think *you're* sexy. And beautiful. And funny." He presses his lips to mine, but doesn't deepen the kiss. "You intrigue me, and that hasn't happened in a very long time, London."

"You're sexy." My voice is breathy. I'm gripping on to his shoulders, my nails barely digging in.

He kisses me now. *Really* kisses me, one hand cupping my jaw and neck as his tongue glides over mine. He nibbles the side of my lips, giving me goose bumps, and then takes my mouth again, as if he's memorizing me.

It's the sexiest kiss I've ever experienced.

When he pulls away, he cups my ass in his hands and smiles down at me. "You have a great ass."

"So do you."

"You noticed?"

"Of course I noticed."

He chuckles and sets me back on the stool.

"I'm starving," he says, returning to the stove to stir the gravy. "And we should have breakfast too, since you went to all of this trouble."

"I have to leave in thirty minutes," I inform him, checking the time.

"Oh? Where to?"

"PT." I load my plate and sit at the table. It's going to be a bitch today, given that I'm already achy. But I refuse to miss any more appointments.

"I have plans with Mom and Gabby this afternoon," he says with a frown.

"That's okay, I have plans too."

He cocks a brow.

"Hey, I have stuff to do. I don't just sit around here and hope to feel better while I pine away for you."

Rather than apologize, he laughs. "I know that. Although,

a little pining might be nice. Okay, tomorrow evening I'd like to have you to myself."

"I can swing that. I'm giving Gabby a lesson tomorrow afternoon. She's excited."

"She's been talking about it for two days," he says with a nod. "Unfortunately, it'll be your first and last lesson because Mom is taking her with her when she leaves tomorrow evening."

"Oh? Gabby doesn't want to stay here anymore?"

"She would rather go to Hawaii with Mom, where she doesn't have to take karate and learn how to ride a horse."

I nod. "I get it. She'll have fun with her grandmother."

"She'll get even more spoiled than she already is."

"That's what grandparents do," I remind him, and feel a moment of sadness that my parents won't get to know the joy of being grandparents. They would have been *awesome* at it.

"What is it?" he asks, but I just shake my head and take a bite of my biscuit. "Will you miss her?"

"Gabby?"

I nod.

"I'll see her back in New York before too long. And no, I won't miss dealing with a hormonal little girl every day."

I laugh and then just smile at him. "You didn't do too bad. How long are you planning to stay before you have to return to New York?"

He frowns, and takes a moment before answering.

"I was supposed to go back the day after tomorrow."

"Oh." I nod, not sure why I'm sad at that. Okay, I know why. We're finally going to have a chance to be alone, and he has to leave. It sucks, big-time.

"But I'm not going to."

My head turns quickly in his direction. "You're not?"

"No, I'm going to stay for a while longer." He leans against the counter and pins me in his dark eyes. "I want more time with you."

"What about work?"

He rubs his hand over his face. "It'll have to wait for me."

"Finn, you shouldn't put your work at risk."

"It'll wait for me," he repeats. "Now, let's eat."

"I'M SO SAD that I only got to sing with you once," Gabby says the next afternoon after we've had an hour-long lesson.

"But you get to go to Hawaii," I say, and give the little girl a hug. "You'll have too much fun to worry about voice lessons."

"Maybe," she replies. "Thank you for today."

"You're welcome. You have a beautiful voice, Gabby. If you keep working on it, you'll be able to do really wonderful things someday."

Her smile is beaming as she walks toward my back door.

"You have to come home with me," she informs me.

"Why?"

"Because you do."

I narrow my eyes. "Why?"

"Because you're supposed to have dinner with Uncle Finn."

"Yes, I'm coming over in a little while. It's only five."

"Will you just trust me?" She rolls her eyes and takes my hand. "Why don't adults just do as they're told?"

I snort out a laugh as she pulls me out the door and down the shortcut path to Finn's house. She's careful not to go too fast so I can keep up with her.

"I think many adults would ask the same question about kids."

"You're going to like this," she promises, and leads me up the deck to the back door and walks inside. There doesn't seem to be anyone home, as the house is quiet, until we get to the living area.

Suitcases are packed and sitting by the front door, and a salt-and-pepper-haired woman is standing with Finn in the living room, fussing over a bouquet of flowers.

"We're here," Gabby announces, and they both turn to look at us.

"Hi. I don't know why I'm here, but Gabby insisted I come with her."

Finn smiles at me and immediately crosses to me to kiss my cheek and thread his fingers through mine.

"This is great, I can introduce you to my mom before she and Gabby take off."

Oh, perfect. I'm meeting the mom.

Talk about nerve-racking.

I paste my professional smile on my face and hold my hand out to shake hers, but she just pulls me in for a big hug.

"Oh, darling, I'm a hugger," she says. "You must be London. I'm Margaret Cavanaugh, Finn's mother."

"So nice to meet you."

She pulls back and gives me a long look. "You're London Watson."

I glance up at Finn. "Yes, I am."

"Oh my goodness, I've seen so many of your plays on Broadway. Why, I've been watching you for *years*. You're a talented young woman."

I feel the glow come over me whenever anyone says they've followed my career. "Thank you very much, Mrs. Cavanaugh."

"Maggie, please," she says, and offers me another hug. "I read about the tragic loss of your parents. I'm so sorry."

"Thank you."

"Our car is here," Gabby says, and throws herself into my arms. I'm getting a lot of hugs today. "Thank you for everything, London. You're awesome."

"You're pretty awesome yourself, kiddo."

Gabby smiles brightly and then gives Finn a hug before whispering in his ear, making him grin.

"I will," he says. "You be good for Grandma, you hear me?"

"She's a perfect angel," Maggie replies with a sniff. "And to insinuate otherwise is offensive."

"Right." Finn rolls his eyes and helps the two women into the car that will take them to the airport. "Have a good flight, and let me know when you get there."

"Grandma's taking us first-class," Gabby says with excitement. "I get anything I want to drink."

"Don't drink too much liquor," I call into the car, making them both laugh. "Have fun!"

And with that, they drive away and Finn and I are left in the house alone.

Finally.

"She's very nice." I don't know what else to say. This is the first time we've been alone without Gabby being nearby or needing Finn's attention and I'm kind of nervous, if the giant butterflies in my stomach are to be believed.

"I like her," he says with a smile, walking slowly toward me. "I have some things for you."

"More than one thing?"

"Yes."

I smile brightly. "I have a love/hate relationship with presents."

"Do you?"

I nod.

"How so?"

"Well, I'm human, so presents are fun."

His lips twitch.

"But sometimes gifts come with strings attached."

His eyes narrow before he takes my hand and leads me into a formal dining room. The table is set with white china and teal linens. Candles are placed around the room and are lit.

"I'll be right back."

He disappears for a second and comes back with the flowers from the living room.

"These are for you."

I sigh and bury my nose in a pink rose, breathing in the scent of them. "Thank you."

"No strings attached with these, they're just beautiful and remind me of you. Do you mind if I put them on the table?"

"Of course not."

He centers them on the beautifully decorated table and then takes my hand and leads me to the kitchen, which smells delicious.

"I've already started cooking," he informs me, and pulls out a stool so I can sit and watch while he continues to work. "I have appetizers done."

He pulls a plate out of the oven and sets it before me, then pulls his phone out, taps the screen, and soft music magically fills the air.

It's pretty damn romantic.

"Clam-and-Gouda-stuffed mushrooms. I also have a charcuterie board with cheeses, meats, nuts, and olives."

"There's going to be *more* food after this?" I stare in amazement at the beautiful array of food, and don't know where to start.

"Of course, but we can take our time." He winks at me. "Are you hungry?"

"Yes. Have you noticed that all we seem to do when we're together is eat?"

"Oh, I think that's about to change," he says, and pulls some steaks out of the fridge. "How was your voice lesson?"

"It was fun. She has a good voice." I pop an olive in my mouth, and then take some salami and cheese. "This is delicious."

"Is it?"

"Come here."

He does as I ask, circling the island to stand next to me, just the way he did yesterday at my house. I offer him some cheese and salami, and he takes the bite directly from my fingers, letting his tongue rest on the pad of my thumb for a moment.

"Delicious," he murmurs, then reaches for a mushroom and holds it up to my lips. I watch him as I take a bite, then let my eyes slide closed as the flavors cover my tongue.

"Oh, that's good."

He leans in and kisses my bare shoulder.

"You know how those noises affect me."

"I can't help it, you keep feeding me wonderful things."

His fingertips wander up and down my arms, making my nipples pucker in anticipation.

"Are you hungry for dinner?"

I shake my head no.

"Excellent."

He leaves me long enough to return the supplies he'd pulled out back to the fridge, and then joins me, boosting me onto the countertop so I'm closer to him.

"I'm real sick and tired of keeping my hands off you, London."

"I don't remember receiving the memo that said you have to keep your hands off me." I hook my foot behind his leg and urge him closer to me.

"I want you."

"I'm right here."

"Once I start, I'm not going to stop."

"Is that a warning?"

"A promise."

I grin and drag my fingers down his cheek. "No objections, Counselor."

Rather than kiss me, his lips land on my neck, where he nibbles and licks his way to my collarbone, making me moan in delight.

"If at any time this makes you uncomfortable, or hurts your leg, I need you to talk to me."

"I'm a talker," I assure him, and grip onto the hair at the back of his head, willing him to never stop the magic that's happening to my neck. He cups my breast over my tank top and flicks his thumb over my nipple, making me bite my lip.

I pull his shirt out of his shorts so I can finally touch the smooth skin there over rock-hard abs. My finger slips between the waistband of his shorts and his skin, and I run it back and forth, making him groan.

"You're making me crazy, baby."

"Isn't that the point?"

His hand glides up my thigh, inside where my core is pulsing with need, and his fingertips brush gently over my shorts, where I need him the most.

"You're so damn warm."

"And wet."

"Fuck."

Chapter Five

~London~

He lifts me off the island and carries me into the living room, where he lays me down on the couch and kneels beside me, his hands all over me, as if he's playing a treasured instrument.

"I need better access to you," he says, and tugs my tank over my head, tosses it over his shoulder, and pauses to nuzzle my breasts over my bra. "You have great breasts."

"Small."

"Responsive." He watches the nipple pucker under the fabric. I arch my back and he unfastens the bra, then tosses that over his shoulder as well, making me laugh. "Fuck, look at you."

I'd rather look at Finn as his eyes roam up and down my torso. He lays his hand over my sternum and then glides down over my navel. I'm slender, but my muscles have lost some of their definition.

From the look on his face, he doesn't mind in the least.

"I took my shirt off, now it's your turn."

His lips twitch with amusement as he grips the shirt between his shoulder blades and gives it a tug, pulling it over his head in that sexy way that men do, and I'm met with bronze, smooth, sexy male skin.

My hand roams over his chest and down his stomach. I can't stop touching him. He leans over me, so my hand slides over his side to his back and his lips lock on a nipple, making my back arch in response.

"Oh, damn," I moan. He alternates from sucking and biting to gently rubbing his tongue over it. It's making me crazy, and this is just a nipple. I can't even imagine what it would feel like if he paid the same attention to my pussy.

Just the thought of it has me scissoring my legs in anticipation.

We both still have our shorts on. My panties are certainly soaked through, and his cock is straining against the material of his shorts.

I want to scream, *Let's get this show on the road! Fuck me!*

But before I can, he lifts me in his arms again and carries me up the stairs to his bedroom.

I haven't been in here before, so I try to get a look around before he lowers me to the bed.

It's a massive room, with large wood furniture and masculine linens.

It looks like him.

He sets me down on the bed and his brown eyes, hot with lust and need, glide over my body. He hooks his fingers into my shorts at my hips and pulls them, along with my panties, down my legs, and tosses them aside.

With his gaze holding mine, he shuffles out of his shorts and, from the end of the bed, crawls up to join me.

But rather than covering me with his body, he lays his hands on my thighs.

"Where should I avoid touching your leg?"

I point to the area that gives me the most trouble, and he presses an openmouthed kiss there before spreading my legs wide, opening me up to him.

"You *are* wet," he says, and slips his finger through the wetness, over my lips and clit. I bite my lip and arch my hips at the same time, silently begging him for more.

"Please."

"Please what?"

I chuckle and grip his hair in my fist, urging him closer.

"I want to hear the words, baby."

"Kiss me."

He plants a kiss on my inner thigh. "Here?"

"No."

He kisses my hip. "Here?"

"You know that's not where I want you."

He blows on my center, but presses a kiss as high up on my thigh as he can go without kissing my pussy.

"Here?" His voice is a gruff whisper now, and I can only

shake my head and grip on to the sheets at my hips. "Fuck, you smell good."

Finally, *finally*, his tongue grazes over my hard clit, and down into my folds, and I let out a long, lusty moan as his mouth does things to me that could possibly be illegal in some states.

Maybe even *this* state.

He pulls my lips into his mouth, hollows his cheeks, and makes a pulsing motion that sends me into a tailspin. My hips are bucking and grinding against him, so hard that he has to cup my ass in his hands to keep me still while he has his way with me.

He presses his thumb against my clit and I come apart, the sky explodes, and I cry out as the orgasm consumes me, until I'm nothing but an exhausted heap when he replaces his mouth with his fingers and climbs over me. I feel him reach to the side of the bed and hear the tear of a condom packet.

"Open your eyes, London."

He's leaning over me, resting on his elbow with one hand in my hair while he takes care of protecting us both with the other. His pelvis is cradled against mine, and his long, hard dick is slipping back and forth against me, reigniting the tingles and sexual energy from a few moments ago.

"I need to be inside you," he says with a whisper. The head of his cock is poised at my very ready pussy. He kisses me gently and my hands roam down his back to his firm ass. "I can't wait to feel you."

"Now," I murmur. "Inside me now."

He needs no further invitation. He presses gently and slides effortlessly into my slick opening, pausing when he's balls-deep, and tips his forehead against mine.

"Jesus Christ," he mutters.

"London," I correct him, and bite his shoulder, which triggers his hips into motion, moving in a long, slow pattern of in and out, pressing against my clit with his pubis every time he's sunk as deep as he can go.

We're nothing but sweaty limbs and heavy breaths and pure lust as he picks up the pace, kissing me deeply as he tips me right over the edge into another orgasm so all-consuming, I don't know where he ends and I begin.

And I don't fucking care.

When I begin to feel my extremities again, Finn rolls off me, keeping me with him and tucking me against his side. We're still panting. I'm pretty sure I'm glowing.

"Hungry?" he asks.

"So hungry," I confirm, and pull away to start searching for my clothes, but he pulls me back to him and kisses me softly.

"Thank you," he murmurs.

"I think I'm the one who came two or three times, so I should be thanking you." I kiss his cheek and roll away, reach for my shorts and pull them on, then simply laugh. "I guess I'll just walk downstairs topless, because I think that's where you left my tank."

"It's going to be a hardship to watch you walk around my house like that," he says as he also pulls on his shorts, takes my hand, and leads me to the stairs. They don't hurt my leg as badly as they did even a week ago, which makes me ridiculously happy. Once I'm back in my bra and tank, we go back to the kitchen and I devour three pieces of cheese, five olives, and a handful of cashews before Finn has the opportunity to take the steaks back out of the oven.

"You *are* hungry," he says with a laugh.

"Worked up an appetite," I reply with my mouth full.

"I'd better get these on the grill, then. You stay here."

I happily boost myself onto a stool and continue munching on the appetizers he made. I can see him through the glass on his deck, standing over the grill in that confident way that men do, wielding a huge spatula while smoke billows around him.

How is it possible that just about everything Finn does is sexy? I mean, he's a human being, so there has to be *something* that will annoy me. Maybe he puts the toilet paper on the thingie wrong. Or doesn't order butter on his popcorn.

What kind of a monster does that?

I've consumed half of the mushrooms when he comes back inside and checks on something in the oven.

"How do you like your steak?" he asks.

"Medium. How do you like your popcorn?"

He turns and frowns in confusion. "Sorry?"

"If you were to go to the movies, how do you order your popcorn?"

He blinks. "Why do I think this is a trick question?"

I smirk and shrug.

"With butter?"

"Is that the real answer, or what you *think* I want to hear?"

"This is more pressure than taking the bar," he says, and rubs his hand over his face. "I have them put butter in the middle and on top."

"Cool."

He laughs and leans in for a smacking kiss. "Why do I feel like I just passed some kind of test?"

"Because you did." I eat another olive. To my surprise, Finn takes my hand and guides me off of the stool, then pulls me into his arms to slow-dance with me in his kitchen. "You're a good dancer."

"Mom insisted when I was a kid." He's holding my hand properly, his other hand is holding the small of my back firmly, and he's smoothly guiding me around the room. "Is this okay?"

"It's great." And I'm thrilled to discover that it's true. My leg isn't bothering me at all. I haven't danced in months, and this is the best gift Finn could have given me.

"You're pretty good at this too," he says. "It's nice to dance with someone who doesn't step on my feet."

"Many, many years of dance under my belt." He twirls me out from him, and then back, holding me closer to his chest. When Adele's song comes to an end, he dips me back dramatically, and then kisses me until I see stars.

That may have been the best dance of my life.

"Perfect timing to flip the steaks," he says, and hurries outside to tend to the grill, and I'm left breathing heavily, my body singing in response to him, wondering how it is that I was lucky enough to have him walk into my life.

Just then, my phone pings on the kitchen counter with a text. Expecting it to be Sasha, I happily pick it up and then frown when I see it's from a number I don't recognize.

> You're such a bitch! I can't believe Mom and Dad left it all to you and I got jack shit. You need to give me some money, L. I'm broke, and I don't have anywhere to go. This is your fault, and you need to fix it.

I sigh and block the number, then delete the message. This is not new. Over the past ten years, my brother has threatened, begged, manipulated, and guilt-tripped me and my parents into giving him many thousands of dollars to feed his drug habit.

I promised myself, and my parents, that I wouldn't do it anymore.

He's been offered a way out, and he refused. I can't, for my own sanity, micromanage him anymore. He doesn't want my help, he wants a handout, and I just can't.

I can't.

Finn walks back in as I set my phone down, and sees the tremble in my fingers.

"What's wrong?"

I shake my head, but he sets the steaks down and leans on the countertop, facing me.

"You did that to me yesterday when I asked you what was bothering you, and I let it pass, but I'm not going to do that this time. This isn't just sex for me, London. I don't know where it might lead, but as far as I'm concerned, I'm in something important here, and that means that it's not all jokes and sexual attraction. I sincerely want to know when something is hurting or bothering you."

Okay. He makes sense. As much as it would make things simpler, it's not just sex for me either, and I would want the same from him. So, I take a deep breath and give him the truth.

"My brother texted." He narrows his eyes and keeps listening. "I'd show it to you, but I deleted it. I blocked the number."

"What did he say?"

His voice is hard, like the day in his office.

"That I need to give him money because I owe him." I shrug and then rub my hands over my face. "Of course I won't send him anything, and he knows what to do to get his inheritance."

"Do you want to talk about this? If it's not something you want to share, it's okay."

"Honestly, I don't feel a lot toward him anymore, which is maybe the saddest part of all. We only have each other now, since our parents are gone, but unless something radical happens and he's willing to make some drastic life changes, he just isn't allowed to be in my life.

"Kyle always had a mean streak, even when we were kids. So, it's not like we were super close and then he became an addict and screwed it all up. He never hurt me, and I still believe that he wouldn't physically hurt me, not when he's sober anyway. But he's the kind of person who gets a kick out of someone hurting. Like, if I didn't get a part I wanted, he'd laugh. That sort of thing.

"And then the drugs started. At first it was alcohol when he was a teenager, and I don't think he's ever been sober since. I'm honestly surprised he's lived this long."

"Me too," Finn says.

"My parents made excuses for him for a long time. Especially my mom. Until finally, after they'd given him seventy-five thousand dollars for rehab and he disappeared with it and just blew it all, probably up his nose or in a vein, they cut him off. I've never seen my mom so devastated."

"So the will didn't surprise you."

"Oh no. Not at all. And I don't feel guilty."

"You shouldn't."

"But five, or even two years ago I would have. And now I'm just numb when it comes to him. He's a manipulator, and he's toxic. So no, he isn't welcome in my life. I do hope he gets help before it kills him, but I wouldn't bet the farm on it."

"That's a tough position to be in," he says as he plates our dinners. It smells and looks absolutely delicious. "I know your father struggled with his decision to have Kyle removed from the will."

"I'm sure he did. My dad was a control freak, and he couldn't control Kyle. But, my parents were good people. Isn't it amazing how two kids can be born of the same couple, raised in the same household, and turn out so differently?"

"It's fascinating," he agrees, leading me into the dining room as he carries our plates. "Wine?"

"No thanks." I cut into my steak and take a bite and can only look at Finn in absolute awe.

"Do you hate it?"

"Oh my God, Finn, this is delicious." I take another bite and sigh with pleasure. "Did you go to culinary school?"

"No," he says with a laugh. "I just cook what I like to eat. And I don't like to eat bad food."

"Well, this is great." There are twice-baked potatoes and asparagus on my plate as well, and I dig in with enthusiasm, already forgetting Kyle's text. "So, how does a successful attorney get to take this much time away from his own firm?"

"I just wrapped up a big case that I'd been working on for about eighteen months. I was exhausted. The great thing about corporate law is, it's mostly a Monday-through-Friday gig, unlike criminal law, which I'm sure you know because your dad was also in the corporate law world."

I nod, and he keeps going.

"But there are still some intense cases, and I just finished one. I was going to head back to the office tomorrow to help my brothers with a couple of their cases, but I have a few months before I have to start the heavy work on my next case, so I've been able to do a lot of work from here, especially since I'm not taking any new clients at this time."

"That's great," I reply. "And it's nice to have a place to get away to, to take you out of the city and away from the root of the stress."

"Is that why you came here?" he asks.

"Part of it," I confirm. "My parents have had this property since before I was born. From what I've heard, Dad got it for a steal and did a ton of remodeling to spruce it all up. So we were here every single summer my entire life. I have a lot of happy memories here, and it's true that I needed to get out of the city. My apartment in Manhattan is convenient to everything that I love, and also a constant reminder that I don't get to live that life right now. I couldn't go to the house in the mountains of North Carolina because that's the house that burned down, and the house in Connecticut is my parents' house. It's where I grew up, my childhood home, and it's *theirs*. Does that make sense?"

"It does." He reaches over and takes my hand in his, holding on tightly.

"So I had my doctor in the city refer me to one here along with a physical therapist, and made the decision to recover here. I still think it was the best decision."

"I am exceedingly thankful that you made that decision," he says, and kisses the back of my hand before turning it over and placing a kiss on my palm. "I was immediately attracted to you that day, and I apologize, because it wasn't really the time or place to hit on you."

"You asked me to dinner," I remind him, earning a sheepish smile. "I was both pissed and flattered."

"Well, I didn't try very hard. You looked so sad. Haunted. And I want to punch the fuck out of Kyle."

"That makes two of us."

"Do you know where he is?"

"No." I shake my head and take my hand back so I can cut my steak. "He's all over the place. I've had calls from L.A., Texas, Florida. I've been told he's spent time in Seattle. He just roams about, he doesn't have a home. And every time he texts or calls it's from a different number.

"I don't even know how the police found him after the fire."

"I'd feel better if we knew where he was," Finn says.

"Why?"

"Because I'd rather know than be surprised."

"Trust me, he won't surprise anyone. I go years without hearing from him." I take a sip of water and another bite of my potato. "It's nice that you're close to your family."

"They're a pain in my ass most days, but yes."

"What are they like?"

"You'll get to see for yourself, I'm sure. Quinn usually comes out here for a week in the summer. He's also pretty much a workaholic, smart. Younger than me by only a year, and swears he's never going to settle down."

"Famous last words." I grin. "And Carter?"

"He's starting to come back around," he replies. "Carter used to be the class clown. Funnier than anyone else I knew. He went to school with Quinn, and started dating Darcy, my sister, in high school. They got married just out of college."

"What happened to her?"

"Cancer," he says with a sigh. "Who would have thought that a thirty-year-old woman could die of breast cancer?"

"I'm so sorry. That's tragic."

"It really was. Carter was completely wiped out. Mom lived with him for about a year so she could take care of Gabby. Not that he was incompetent, he was just so *lost*."

"That's horrible," I murmur.

"This has been a pretty heavy conversation," Finn says as he pushes his empty plate away. "Maybe we should lighten it up a bit."

"What do you have in mind?"

"Follow me."

Chapter Six

~Finn~

I hold my hand out for London's and smile when she reaches for me and follows me through the kitchen to a room that's tucked behind it.

"I didn't know this was back here," she says. "You have a playroom."

I cross my arms over my chest and watch as London wanders through the room, running her fingers over the pool table, the Ping-Pong table, checking everything out.

"You want to play pool?" she asks.

"I was thinking pinball," I reply, and walk to the vintage machine in the corner of the room. "I can pull a stool up for you if you like."

"I'm feeling pretty good," she says. "And I have to warn you; I'm very, *very* good at pinball."

"Is that right?" I push the button behind the machine that

launches the ball without having to put quarters in. "Should I be scared?"

"Maybe," she says as I stand aside so she can go first. She pulls back the lever and lets go, propelling the ball in the machine, and for the next few minutes doesn't miss a trick. Her reflexes are on point, her tongue bitten between her teeth as she plays, and when she does lose the ball, she pouts.

Adorably.

"Your turn," she says, and steps aside. I take my place, set the ball in motion, and just when it reaches the paddle at the bottom, London pulls my hand off the button so I can't hit it. "Oh, that's too bad."

"Are you kidding me?"

"I must have slipped," she says with a shrug, and pushes me out of the way so she can play again. Her tongue is caught between her teeth again, her blue eyes following the ball intently, and I can't take my eyes off her.

Her body is simply amazing. Slightly curvy, but toned and so fucking responsive to me that it's intoxicating. Her long dark hair begs for my fingers. And I'm always finding something new, like a small scar behind her knee and the birthmark on her ass.

I think I'll bite her there later.

"Damn it," she says when she loses her ball. "Your turn."

"No slips of the hand this time," I warn her with narrowed eyes, and step up to take my turn. I'm about thirty seconds in when she plants her foot behind my knee, making my leg give out, and I lose the ball. "Seriously?"

"Are you okay?" she asks with wide eyes. "It looked like your knee buckled or something."

"Yeah, because you pushed it."

"I wouldn't do that."

I lean in and kiss her. "You're a dirty cheater."

"Me?"

"You're the only other one here."

"I don't know what you're talking about, but if it makes you feel better, you can take another turn."

I laugh and step back, hands in the air. "No, you take another turn, hotshot. I'll be right back."

"I'll be a while," she says with a sassy grin, and turns her back to me so she can go to work on some pinball.

I shake my head and walk to the kitchen. I pull the crème brûlée my mom prepared earlier today out of the fridge and sprinkle sugar on top, fire up the blowtorch, and melt it down to a hard, golden brown. Placing the dishes on a tray, I make two decaf coffees, adding a little sugar and cream, add them to the tray, and after grabbing spoons and napkins, I carry it all into the playroom to find London bouncing and yelling at the machine.

"Take that, you motherfucker," she says, her voice fierce. "I've got you now."

"This isn't the pinball Olympics," I remind her, and set the tray on the table beside her. "You're not in the running for a medal or anything."

"I might be a little competitive," she replies, and then sighs when the ball slips by her. "Damn it."

"Take a break." I show her the dessert and hold a chair out for her. "Join me for something sweet."

"You feed me *all the time*," she says as she cracks into her dessert. "I haven't eaten this good in years."

"It's just crème brûlée and coffee."

"And it's delicious." She takes another bite and then a sip of her coffee. "I should probably go home after this."

"Why?"

She stops and meets my gaze, her spoon in her mouth. "Because I live there?"

"Do you have something pressing to do?"

"No."

"Is it locked up?"

"Of course."

"I want you to stay." I offer her a bite on my spoon and she takes it. "I'd like to get naked with you again. Hold you while you sleep."

I take a bite.

"I'd like to be with you tonight."

"You're not sick of me already?"

I take a moment to answer because I don't want to sound too eager. "No. I don't see a time in my near future that I'll be *sick* of you."

"Well, then I'll stay."

She takes a bite as if she's just told me that she'd like another cup of coffee. As if it's not a big deal at all.

Maybe it's not a big deal for her, but it's not small for me. I don't sleep over with women. I don't invite them into my home for meals and games and sex.

I don't do this, yet I can't stay away from London.

"Thank you."

She finishes her crème brûlée and then smiles at me. "You're welcome. Now, if I beat you at pinball, you have to stay naked for the rest of the evening."

"What if I win?"

"Don't be ridiculous, you're not going to win."

I laugh as I join her at the machine. "If you're going to keep cheating, I'm not making this bet."

"I don't cheat," she insists. "And you might want to go to the doctor to get your equilibrium checked out because you almost *fell*."

"Or, you know, you almost pushed me down."

"I have no idea what you're talking about."

I WAKE UP and reach for her in the dark, but the sheets are cool where she was lying not long ago.

She's not here.

I sit up in my bed and rub my hands over my face, then look around the room and pause when I find her.

She's sitting on the floor in front of the glass door that leads out to my deck, her knees pulled up to her chest and arms wrapped around them, a blanket wrapped around her. Her nose is practically pressed to the glass.

I reach for another throw blanket, and rather than ask her to get up and come back to bed, I sit behind her, wrap the blanket around us both, and pull her against my chest while I breathe her in.

"Are you okay?" I whisper in her ear.

"Storm's coming in," she whispers back. Her eyes are wide as she avidly watches the wind push through the trees. Lightning strikes out at sea, lighting everything up and making London flinch. "I don't like storms."

"I've got you," I murmur, and kiss her shoulder.

"Did you see the water?" she asks. "When the lightning struck, did you see how choppy it was?"

"Yes."

"I hope there aren't any ships out there," she says as the thunder booms and she flinches again. "Seaside storms are so crazy. Violent. Angry. Like a woman who's royally pissed off and she doesn't care who knows it."

"That's a good analogy," I reply. "It does look like someone is having a tantrum."

"And it's destructive," she adds.

"What is it about the storm that scares you?"

"Everything. The wind is wild, it could easily pull something out to sea. The rain isn't a sprinkling, but more like God is dumping a huge bucket of water all at once. And the lightning and thunder just tips it all into crazy town. It's loud and bright and messy."

"Sounds like life, if you're living it right," I reply, and kiss her cheek when she glances back at me. "And sometimes that can be scary too."

"This is a deep conversation during a crazy storm."

Lightning flashes overhead, and almost immediately thunder claps, and she turns to bury her face in my chest.

She's the strongest woman I've met in a very long time, and this storm has her reduced to shivering like a child.

"Hey," I murmur, and tip her chin up to look at me. "You can't control the storm, London. It's going to happen whether you're scared, or not. But you can calm yourself in it. That's the trick."

"I've never been good at that," she confesses. "I can't sleep through it, and I feel like I have to watch every second of it, in case something horrible happens and I have to run."

I brush her hair off of her cheek and hook it behind her ear.

"Nothing horrible is going to happen tonight," I assure her. "In fact, I think some wonderful things are going to happen."

"Really?" Her voice and eyes tell me she doesn't believe me, so I just lower my mouth to hers and kiss her deeply, soaking in every moment with her. She shivers when my fingers drift from her neck, over her collarbone, to her breast, and it's not from the storm, but from my touch.

She comes alive when I touch her and it's fucking amazing.

"That feels nice," she says before swallowing hard and turning to me fully now, naked beneath our blankets, a tangle of legs and quiet breaths.

"You're beautiful, London. I find it very difficult to keep my hands to myself."

"No need," she says as her eyes drift closed and she leans into my touch. She lets the blanket fall and reaches out to run her fingers down my chest, not stopping until her hand is wrapped around my fully erect cock. She pumps it slowly but firmly and I want to jerk her onto me and have my way with her.

But that's not what this moment is all about.

It's about forgetting, and discovering new memories.

Before I can lay her down and touch every inch of her with my mouth, she leans down and brushes her tongue around the rim of my cock, barely touching me but setting me on fire.

Just when I think I can't take any more, she slides that sweet mouth over me, then pulls up and just barely scrapes her teeth over my skin, and I can't sit still anymore.

I sink my fingers into her hair, gripping hard as she works me over. I can feel the tightening in my balls, the humming in the base of my spine, and I know that if she doesn't stop *right now*, I'm going to come in her mouth.

And as much as I don't hate that idea, that's not what I want right now.

"London." My voice is gruff, and she doesn't respond to me, so I tug her up and off of me, stand, and lift her in my arms, carrying her back to the bed.

"I want to be on you," she says, her voice sure and strong.

"I won't argue with that." I kiss her, letting my lips slip and move over hers as she pushes my shoulders back, urging me to lie down in the middle of the bed. She reaches for a condom, and swiftly rolls it down my length, making my eyes cross. "Christ almighty."

"I can't tell you how good it feels to be able to do this." She holds me at the opening of her pussy, and slowly lowers herself onto me. Her hands are braced on my chest and she starts to rock back and forth. "I couldn't sit like this a few weeks ago, and I can do it. It doesn't hurt."

"This should never hurt, sweetheart."

She smiles down at me, rocking, barely moving me in or out of her, but she's rubbing her clit against my pubis, and her muscles are quivering.

Fuck, I've never seen anything more beautiful than London looking down at me, the lightning flashing and then leaving her in shadows again.

"Keep talking," I urge her, enjoying the sound of her voice.

"You fill me," she murmurs, and leans down, covering me, and placing her lips next to my ear. "You fill me up, Finn. It makes my body feel hot. Sexy."

"You *are* sexy."

"Powerful," she says, and bites my earlobe, and I can't take it anymore. I grip her ass in my hands and roll us, avoiding her bad leg, tucking her under me.

She lifts her knees, opening herself even wider, and I press down, holding myself inside her. She rests her right ankle on my shoulder. I turn my head and bite her ankle, then press openmouthed kisses there.

"I thought I was going to be on top," she says, grinning up at me.

"I couldn't help it." I press my thumb to her clit and smile in satisfaction when she arches her back, tilting her hips and pressing herself even more firmly against me. "You turn me inside out, London. I needed this, to look down at you while I'm inside you. Trust me, you're no less powerful."

"I know." She licks her fingers and brushes my hand away so she can touch herself. I pull back just an inch and she lets her fingertips glide against my slick cock, wet from her juices, while she presses against her clit. Her womb clenches even tighter around me, and I know that I'm not going to last.

I can't keep my hips from moving faster, pushing harder, taking this moment from soft and quiet to fast and urgent, chasing the incredible orgasm that I can feel building in both of us.

Finally, London's whole body trembles and she cries out as she lets go, riding the waves of lust and desire, and I happily go over with her.

I gingerly pull out of her and fall to her side, tugging her against me as we try to catch our breath. My eyes are heavy. I want to slide into a deep, satisfied sleep, but London shifts next to me and props her head on her hand, her hair falling around us both.

"Are you tired?" she asks.

"Aren't you?"

She just shrugs, which is womanspeak for *no*. She's back to thinking about the storm.

"I think it's calming down out there," I assure her, and cup her face, rubbing her cheek with my thumb.

"Maybe."

"It's almost time for the sun to come up." She leans in and kisses me sweetly. "Does this mean we aren't going back to sleep tonight?"

"I'm sorry," she says.

"No need to be sorry." I stand from the bed and pull on some sweatpants and a T-shirt, and rummage in my drawer for a clean tee and shorts with a drawstring for London, then pass them to her. "These might work."

"Thanks." She wiggles into them, and makes me laugh. "I look homeless."

"You don't look homeless." I take her hand and lead her downstairs. "You look like you're wearing your lover's clothes because yours are dirty."

"Well then, it's an accurate look."

I lead us through the kitchen and to the breakfast nook that looks out at the ocean. The table is small, but the chairs are deep and comfortable. I get London settled in a chair, then run to the TV room to grab a throw blanket and drape it over her.

"You're spoiling me," she says with a smile, holding the blanket close to her. "And I kind of like it."

"Good. I'm going to make you coffee."

"Having you around is handy," she says, and smiles when I turn away, shuffling into the kitchen. When the coffees are made, and I've toasted some bagels and set some jam and cream cheese on the tray, I walk back to the table and set it out. She's quietly watching the horizon, worrying her bottom lip in her teeth.

"The storm has passed." I sit and offer her the coffee, which she gratefully accepts.

"And the sunrise is gorgeous," she adds. "My dad and I would do this when I was young. Sit out after a storm to watch the sunrise."

"That's a nice storm memory."

"You've given me more," she says, glancing at me when she reaches for a bagel and cream cheese. "Thank you for that."

"Making love with you is never a chore," I reply, causing her to smirk.

"I should hope not. But you've given me another happy storm memory, and I am grateful." She takes a bite. "Look at that water."

"It's amazing to me that the wind can be gone, and the rain has passed, and yet the water is still so churned up."

"It brings so many interesting things to shore," she says, her eyes almost excited now.

"Why do I think that we're about to go on an early-morning beachcombing mission?"

"Because we are." She takes a sip of her coffee and sits back in her chair, her legs tucked up against her chest again. "But first I want to sit here, in this comfortable chair, with this comfortable man, and enjoy the view."

"First you call me *nice* and now you call me *comfortable*. You're not great for a man's ego."

"Something tells me you don't need me to stroke your ego, Finn Cavanaugh," she replies, watching me over the rim of her mug. "And you know what else is awesome?"

"What?"

"I can sit with my knees up. Finally. Without it killing my leg."

"You're healing, London. That's amazing."

"I didn't know if I ever would, and I don't just mean my leg, you know. But I'm feeling better. Like there might be hope at the end of this long road."

"What else is at the end of it?"

"Normalcy. Work, if I'm lucky."

"And?"

"Well, it's convenient that we live in the same city, because I'd like to continue to have you in my life after we leave here."

"We're on the same page there."

"Good." She smiles and takes a bite of her bagel. "Let's go look for cool shit on the beach, as soon as I finish eating this."

"Sounds like an excellent plan."

Chapter Seven

~London~

*S*o, let me get this straight," Sasha says several hours later, after I've gone home to shower and freshen up. "You're having an affair with your dad's estate attorney?"

"That makes it sound . . . shady," I reply, and wrinkle my nose. I pour myself some iced tea and sit on the sun porch. "I mean, yeah, he handled the estate, but he's also the neighbor."

"Okay, and he's hot?"

"So hot," I confirm. "And he's *so nice*."

"Run. Nice guys don't really exist. They pretend to be nice until they get you hooked, and then the *real* guy comes out and it's all bullshit."

"I don't know, I think this might be the unicorn guy. He's not late when he says he's going to be somewhere, he has a work ethic, loves his family. Oh, and last night when I was freaking out about the storm, he totally calmed me down and we had super-sexy sex to get my mind off of it."

"So he comforted you."

"Yeah. And it was nice."

She's quiet for a moment. "I want to meet him before I make any judgments. Because you could just be infatuated with his niceness and big dick, and maybe I'll see that not only does he have a big dick, but he *is* a big dick."

"You make me laugh so hard," I reply, chuckling. "Of course you'll get to meet him. We went for a walk on the beach this morning to see what the storm brought in and it was so cool. We found some garbage, of course, and a couple of animal carcasses."

"Super romantic," she says, sarcasm dripping from her voice.

"But we also found a piece of a boat. It looked really old, and I think it was part of a shipwreck, and just got washed up."

"Maybe it was a pirate ship. Did you see Captain Jack Sparrow?"

"You're in a bitchy mood this morning," I reply, and sip my drink, then notice the door to the playhouse open. "Who peed in your Cheerios today?"

"I'm sorry, I'm just jealous. You're frolicking on the beach with a sexy dude and I'm working my ass off in the city. The weather has been shit, especially for summer, and the director of this new play is determined to kill me. I'm tired and bitchy, and I'm sorry."

"It's okay. The first few weeks of a new show are always the worst," I remind her. I remember all too well, and it's one of the things that I don't miss.

"I know. It'll get better once I memorize all of the lines and the marks."

"So, not to change the subject, but you're going with me out to the playhouse in my backyard."

"You have a playhouse?"

"Yeah, my dad had it built for me when I was a little girl. The door is open, and I need to check it out."

"What if there's a madman waiting for you in there?"

"Well, if that's the case, I'll need you to hang up and call 911." I poke my head inside. "Hello?"

"I'm here."

"No, I was calling out into the playhouse." I laugh and step inside. "The storm must have blown the door in. Finn's niece was out here the other night, and I must not have shut the door firmly when we left." I glance around and sigh. "Damn, the wind did a number on this place."

"Is it ruined?"

"No, but stuff is blown over, messed up. I think I'll just shut the door behind me and pretend like it isn't here for now."

I do just that and walk back to the house.

"Maybe I'll come to that house with you sometime," Sasha says with a sigh. "It sounds so nice to get out of the city and relax for a while."

"When you get a break from the show, we'll definitely come here. And if I'm not available, you're always welcome to use it without me."

"Thanks," she says. "When are you coming home?"

"Soon," I reply, and sit back in my favorite chair on the porch. "I don't know exactly when yet, but I'm feeling better and better every day. Recovery is finally happening more rapidly, and although I do love it here, I miss you and the city. But I'm enjoying Finn, so I'm not in a huge hurry."

"I get it," she says, and then yawns. "And I'm so glad you're feeling better. You sound *so good*. It makes me happy."

"I'm pretty happy," I confirm. "Is that bad? I mean, my parents have been gone for less than four months, and my career as I know it may be over. Is it wrong that I'm happy?"

"What are you supposed to do, London? Be miserable for the rest of your life? You're only thirty-two, with a lot of life ahead. So no, I don't think it's bad that you're healing. Grief is a process, and you're processing. I think you sound healthy."

"Thanks." My glass is empty. I pull my knees up to my chest and feel the pull of tired, sore muscles.

But not sore because I'm injured. Sore because I spent the night having sex with maybe the sexiest man I've ever met in my life.

"Oh, one more thing about Finn; he's almost forty."

"That explains it," Sasha says, and I can hear her snap her fingers in the background. "He's older, so he has his shit together. Younger guys don't have their shit together."

"Most don't," I agree. "But not all men are like that. Finn thought that I might have an issue with the age difference."

"Why? You're not a minor."

"That's what I said. It's not like I'm thirty and he's seventy. That might give me pause."

"Ew. That *should* give you pause. Does he have any gray hair?"

"No."

"Too bad. I like a silver fox. That salt-and-pepper-hair thing is sexy."

"Maybe you should date an older guy," I reply with a laugh. "But no, he has dark hair, no gray that I've noticed, and dark brown eyes. Olive skin. I think his family is Italian."

"That's kind of hot. Does he speak Italian?"

"I don't know. I'll have to ask him."

"When are you going to see him again?"

"Later today. I think it's safe to say that I have a massive crush on him. But I think it's more than that too."

"It's about time you fell in love," she says, and I can hear the satisfied smile on her gorgeous face.

"I didn't say love."

"It's okay if you're still in denial. Enjoy your sexy, older lawyer. Fuck him all day long. Let him spoil you a bit."

"I plan to do all of that," I say. "I'll talk to you tomorrow?"

"Same bat time, same bat channel."

"You're doing so great," Joe says at physical therapy a week later. "How does this feel?"

He stretches my leg up by my head.

"It doesn't hurt," I reply, close to tears. I don't understand why today has been so emotional for me at therapy. One minute I'm happy with my progress, and the next I want to break down into ugly sobs. "My muscles are tight because I've lost some of the flexibility, but I don't feel injured."

"Fantastic, kiddo." He runs me through a series of exercises, watching me like a hawk. "That last lunge looked a little shaky."

"Yeah, because I did thirty of them," I reply, and shake my head. "I'm not training for the Olympics here."

"True. And your strength has increased nicely. I'm very happy with your progress, London. You should be proud."

"I am." I blink rapidly and look down, but he catches my chin in his fingers and makes me look at him.

"What's up with the tears today?"

"It feels different." I shrug a shoulder, glance out the window that faces the water, and then back to Joe, who's become more than a therapist. He's my friend.

"How so?"

"I just . . ." I swallow hard. "It feels like things are changing with my body, *and* with how I feel about everything that happened. When you stretch me out, I want to cry. When I lunge, I feel proud, and angry at the same time."

"Why angry?"

"Because my parents can't lunge. They can't do *anything*. But I'll be damned if I'll let the fire kill all of us, especially if I'm still living. So I'm proud, and I'm sad because I miss them."

"They'd be *so proud* of you, London." Joe pats my shoulder and waits while I brush a tear from my cheek. "You're healing. Let's go to my office."

I follow behind him to his office and sit across from him,

snagging a tissue from the box on his desk and wiping my eyes.

"You've held a lot of your grief in your body, London."

I nod, unable to answer at first. "I hold most emotions in my body. It's why dance was always so important to me."

He leans forward, listening avidly.

"I express myself in dance, in music. I haven't been able to use that as my outlet for this grief, for the sadness. But the therapy has helped."

"I'm glad." He smiles and opens the folder sitting on his desk. "And I have some exciting news."

"What?"

"Well, I'm happy to report that I think our time together is done."

I stare at him in disbelief.

"I know, you're gonna miss me, but I don't think there's any reason for you to keep coming here, unless you start having issues again, or feel like you're sliding backward. But you're a strong woman, who was in excellent health to begin with, which helped you immeasurably."

"You're discharging me?"

"Yes, ma'am." He folds his hands on his desk and smiles at me. "Congratulations, London, you've graduated from PT."

I smile and clap my hands, tears threatening again, but happy tears this time. "Awesome. Can I start going to the gym?"

"I don't see why not. Take it easy and listen to your body. Don't overdo it."

"I won't. I'm just ready to get back into decent shape."

"You don't consider this decent shape?" He laughs and shakes his head.

"Joe, I was a professional dancer. I'm twenty pounds heavier and can't run five miles without feeling like I'm going to die."

"I get it. You'll get all of that back. It won't take long."

I nod and stand when he does. I can't help from reaching out and hugging him hard.

"Thank you."

"You're welcome." He pulls back and smiles down at me. "You're going to be great."

I nod and leave the PT office, and when I get to my car, I reach for my phone and immediately call Finn.

"This is Finn."

"Hey, are you busy?"

"Never too busy for you. What's up?"

"I have super-awesome news, and I need to see you right away. Can I come over?"

"Of course. See you soon?"

"Very soon." I hang up and drive directly to his house. I hurry inside and find him in his office at the top of the stairs. "Hi."

"Hey beautiful." He stands and holds his arms open, inviting me in for a hug, and I swear it's like coming home. "Your body is humming. What's going on?"

"I have the best news ever. I've been discharged from PT." I pull back and do a little dance in excitement. "I get to go to the gym and lose the weight I've gained. I can do pretty much whatever I want."

"That's the best news I've had all day," he says, his handsome smile wide and happy. "Not that you're losing weight, but that you're healing. The curves don't bother me."

"The curves don't bother me either, I just want to go to the gym," I reply honestly. "I need to be more active than I have been. Exercise has always come easy to me, and it's time to get back there."

"Anything that puts this glow on your face makes me happy as well," he says. "And I might have an idea on how we can celebrate."

"How?"

"Let's go to London."

I stop and stare at him in confusion. "As in, England?"

"Yes, that one." He leans in to kiss me softly. "To be fair, I'd already planned the trip as a surprise, and this is the perfect opportunity to tell you about it."

"When are we leaving?"

"Tomorrow morning."

I feel my eyes grow wide, and then I smile and launch myself into his arms. "You're taking me to London?"

"Baby, I'll take you anywhere you want."

"Let's start with London." I kiss him and grin when he sits me down on his desk. "This is the best surprise."

"Just wait until you see what I've planned for us there."

THE LIGHTS. THE music, and the dancing. The incredible acting, direction, costuming.

The story.

Finn brought me to London yesterday, first-class, and tonight he brought me to a show at the Bush Theatre, in the West End theater district, London's equivalent to Broadway.

Our seats are, of course, stellar, and all I can do is hold his hand as I sit and take it all in avidly, soaking in every minute of it.

Oh, how I've missed this. Not just being a part of it, but being a lover of the theater, part of the audience, experiencing the absolute magic of what the actors create.

For two hours, we are entertained impeccably, and with each curtain call, I'm on my feet, enthusiastically applauding the hard work of everyone involved.

"What did you think?" Finn asks when the houselights come up.

"Absolutely wonderful," I reply with a wide smile, and crook my finger, silently asking him to lean in and kiss me.

Which he happily does.

"I know some of the cast. Do you mind if we go backstage?"

"Not at all. I'd called ahead, so they're expecting you."

I stare at him in awe for a moment. "You thought to let them know I was coming?"

"Sweetheart, do you know who you are? You're London Watson, and trust me when I say, no one has forgotten that."

Tears spring to my eyes, and all I can do is take a deep breath and squeeze his hand gratefully.

"Let's go," he whispers in my ear, and leads me to the back of the house, where a security guard checks our IDs, then gestures for us to go behind stage where the actors are gathered, signing autographs and greeting fans.

When Jeffrey Cameron, a superstar in both film and stage, sees me from across the room, he poses for one more selfie, then marches over to me and lifts me up in a tight hug.

"How are you, darling?" he asks as he sets me on my feet. "I've been worried sick."

"I'm better," I reply with a smile, and cup his cheek in my hand. "And I've missed you."

"I've been here, doing this show for about six weeks. I have two more weeks to go, and then I head back to the States, and I was going to call you, but now I can talk to you in person."

I frown. "About what?"

"Let's go to my dressing room." He winks at me, and I immediately reach for Finn's hand.

"Jeffrey, I'd like to introduce you to Finn. He brought me here tonight."

"Well, then he's a friend of mine already," Jeffrey says with a perfect smile, and holds his hand out to Finn. "Nice to meet you. I'm Jeffrey Cameron."

"Pleasure," Finn says, but his eyes say that he's not pleased with how familiar Jeffrey is with me.

I'll explain to him later that he has absolutely nothing to worry about.

We're led to Jeffrey's dressing room, and once we're inside with the door closed, he gestures for us to have a seat.

"What's going on?" I ask.

"A movie," Jeffrey replies, and leans forward, his blue eyes dancing in excitement. "I know you've always been content in New York, but I also know that circumstances have changed. There's a new movie that I'm working on with Gerald Silverman."

My eyes widen at the mention of the famous director's name.

"It's amazing, Lon. It's a musical, and I'm the lead male. I need a wife."

I feel Finn stiffen next to me, and I smile up at him. "A movie wife," I clarify.

"That's right. The part is gritty, and real, and the score is out of this world. We're talking Oscar-winning material here, babe."

"I'd have to have my agent request an audition."

"You don't need an audition," Jeffrey says. "If you want the role, we'll fly out to L.A. and read together for Gerald, just to make sure it's right. But I'm telling you, it's right."

"Have you two worked together before?" Finn asks.

"A few times," I confirm. "We work very well together."

"And if I wasn't gay, I'd marry her in a heartbeat," Jeffrey adds with a smile. "I'm telling you, London, this would be an amazing way to get started in film."

"Well, there's a lot to think about." I look up at Finn, who just smiles and offers a shrug.

"Don't look at me, I think you should at least think about it."

And just like that, for the first time since before the fire, I feel the warm glow inside me start to take shape, the way it did before where my career was concerned. I see an opportunity that feels *real*.

"I'll think about it," I reply with a nod, and Jeffrey immediately pulls me in for a bone-crushing hug.

"Excellent," he says. "I'll have the script sent to you so you can look it over, and when I'm back in the States, we will arrange to get with Gerald for a reading."

I nod, a bit shell-shocked, and spend the next thirty minutes chatting about the business, my time on Martha's Vineyard, and Finn tells Gerald about his job and other interests.

It feels so good for Finn to meet someone from my world. Since he will never meet my family, this is as close to that as it gets for me.

Shortly after I say good-bye to Jeffrey, Finn and I are in the backseat of the car he hired, snuggled up, and my mind is whirling with so much information I can't even talk.

Once we're inside our hotel suite, I walk into the bedroom to remove my jewelry and shoes, and then stare at myself in the mirror.

Finn knew that I didn't have clothes appropriate for the theater with me on the island, so he had a beautiful dress and shoes ordered for me.

He also gave me a stunning necklace and earring set made of rubies and yellow gold.

He took me to London, to the theater, and has indulged my every whim since we left the house yesterday.

I wanted to nap, so we napped.

I wanted a grilled cheese sandwich, so he ordered room service.

I leave the bedroom, in search of the very special man that has come into my life, and find him in the sitting room, reading something on his phone.

"Is everything okay?" I ask.

"Yes and no," he replies, then shuts the screen off and sets it aside. "Everything with you is amazing. But there are some things at work that need my attention."

"I've kept you away too long."

I sit next to him and he pulls me into his arms and kisses my forehead.

"I've been exactly where I wanted to be, London. But, once we leave here, I'll have to go to New York."

"Oh." I don't know why I feel so disappointed. I knew our time on Martha's Vineyard wouldn't last forever. No one lives in a bubble. "I have some things to finish up on Martha's Vineyard, and then I'll go to the city as well."

"You don't have to cut your time there short because of me."

I smile up at him and drag my fingertips down his cheek, enjoying the scratchiness of the whiskers that have grown since this morning.

"It's time, I miss the city," I reply simply. "And if you don't mind, I'd like to be able to see you on a regular basis."

"That doesn't bother me in the least."

"Finn." I turn on the couch so I can fully see him. "Thank

you. For this trip, for tonight, and for everything that's come before this."

"London—"

"Let me finish." I take his hand in mine and he kisses my knuckles, bringing the butterflies in my stomach to life. "To be understood is profound. You understand me. It's a big deal."

His lips twitch in that way they do when he's particularly pleased with me and kisses my hand again.

"You're a big deal," he whispers. "And not because of who you are in the show-business community, but because of who you *are*."

I lean into him and sigh when he loops his arms around me and holds on tightly.

"Back at you," I reply happily. "Right back at you."

Chapter Eight

~London~

My phone is ringing.

I rub my eyes as I roll over in bed and reach for my cell, happy to see that it's Finn FaceTiming me.

"Hey," I say, and push my hair out of my eyes.

"Good morning," he says with a smile. He's already dressed in his suit, clean-shaven, looking ridiculously handsome. "I'm sorry I woke you."

"What time is it?"

"A little after nine." I sit up and blink, trying to push the fog from my brain. "Were you up late?"

"Yeah, I started reading a book and couldn't put it down. But it's good you called, because I have to get up and around here, since I'm coming home later today."

"Thank God," he says, watching me avidly. "A week without you has been too long."

I smile and tilt my head. "It *has* been a lonely week," I agree. "But I'll be home in less than twelve hours."

"Do you need anything?"

Just you.

"I don't think so. I have to meet with Tony, the caretaker, in a little bit and finish packing up. Oh, and I have to clean the playhouse."

"What happened in the playhouse?"

"The storm last week did a number on it. I just want to straighten it up and make sure nothing is ruined before I close it up for the year."

"Okay." He looks up and speaks to someone I can't see. "What time does your plane get in?"

"I land at around four. I'll be home by about five thirty."

"Do you mind if I come over after work?"

"I'd be disappointed if you didn't," I reply. "I'll shoot over my address and let the doorman know I'm expecting you."

"Sounds good. Safe travels, baby."

"See you soon."

I hang up and climb out of bed, strip the linens and put them in the washing machine, then get in the shower.

An hour later, I'm dressed and my essentials are packed and sitting by the front door. The next project is cleaning out the fridge, which I hate. But I graze as I pull out bagels and fruits, vegetables, and a questionable container full of something that I don't remember making.

By the time that's finished, I'm full *and* the kitchen is clean.

Multitasking is totally my thing today.

The doorbell rings, and I answer, happy to see Tony. He's worked for my parents since I was a kid.

"Hello, Mr. Tony."

He gives me a hug and takes his hat off as he steps inside.

"How are you, London?"

"I'm doing great," I reply honestly. "I don't know what kind of conversation you and my dad had each year when we left, so you're going to have to help me out here."

"I'm happy to," he says with a shy smile. "I come once a week to mow the grass, trim trees, just landscape in general. I also make a quick stop by a couple of times a week to make sure that the house is soundly locked, and no alarms are going off. I'll clean and cover the pool today, since no one will be using it for some time."

"That all sounds great. I'd also appreciate it if you'd keep an eye on the playhouse. I have a suspicion that there might have been a squatter there for a bit."

He scowls. "I don't see how that's possible. I check the whole property several times a week."

"I'm sure you do, I just wanted to mention it to you, just in case. My neighbor's daughter mentioned seeing a man living out there, and I admit it spooked me."

"Well, I'll pay extra attention to that, and call the police if I see anything. Oh, and I'll keep tabs on the car, check the oil, start it up, that sort of thing so the next time you come, it's ready for you."

"Thank you so much. Tony, I saw in my father's records how much he paid you monthly, and I'd like to continue that pay schedule if that's okay with you."

"Of course," he says. "Although I always told your dad that he paid me too much."

"And I was going to suggest a raise," I reply with a laugh. "You do so much for me here, I'd be happy to pay you more."

"No, this is fair, and I'm happy. If that changes, I'll be sure to let you know. Give me a week or so notice the next time you'll be here, and I'll make sure the house is stocked and ready to go."

"You're wonderful, Tony. Thank you."

Once he's left, I look at the time, and figure I have about two hours until the car will be here to get me, so I grab a couple of large garbage bags and head out to the playhouse.

I was hoping that I'd open the door, and everything would be back in its place again, but no such luck. The toy kitchen is tipped over, all of the plastic plates and foods are all over the floor. The little dining table is on its side, and the small twin mattress is off the bed and on the floor.

This seems like a lot of damage from wind, but it was a crazy storm.

I spend an hour righting everything, throwing away things that were damaged from the water, and make sure that it doesn't need any repairs.

Thankfully, it's just the stuff inside that got broken or messed up.

Once that's finished, I wander down to the beach, but rather than looking out to sea, I turn and look at the huge house that's been left to me.

I love it, but part of me wonders if I should sell it. I know it's worth a fortune, not that I need the money. It's just so *big,* and I'm just me. I don't have kids to bring here, and I don't have a large extended family who could use it.

Maybe I should sell it to a family, and let the house be loved the way it should be.

I glance over at Finn's house and smile. It's not much smaller than mine. If I sold this house, I wouldn't have Finn as a neighbor anymore, and that would be disappointing.

I shrug and turn to walk down the beach. I don't have to make any decisions about it today. Maybe I'll see how the next couple of years go, and how often I actually come here to use it, before I decide on whether to keep it or not.

One thing I do know is, I couldn't be more excited to be going home. Not only do I get to see Finn today, but I've missed my condo, the restaurants I love, and my friends.

I'm ready to get back to my life.

He's on his way over *right now.*

Today might have been the longest travel day in the history of travel days, and the flight was only an hour long. But it was delayed, and then delayed again, and by the time I got my luggage, caught a cab, and made it to my condo in Manhattan, it was after seven in the evening.

Thankfully, Finn ended up working late, so the timing worked out.

But now I'm home, and he's on his way, and I might be acting like a sixteen-year-old on prom night.

I've checked my hair three times, unpacked in record time, and have been pacing around my living room for twenty minutes.

But finally, the bell rings.

"I have a Finn Cavanaugh here for you, Miss Watson," Jerry, the doorman, says. I told him Finn was coming, but they still always announce visitors.

"Great, send him up," I reply, and wait by the door until I hear footsteps coming down the hallway. I open the door, and when Finn appears, I launch myself into his arms, holding on tightly. He shuts the door behind him, presses me against it, and kisses me like his life depends on it.

Thank the good lord.

"Missed you," he murmurs as his lips move from my mouth to my jawline. "So much."

"I missed you too." My fingers dive into his hair and hold on tight as his mouth does amazing things to my neck. "That feels good."

I feel him smile against me, and then he lowers me to the floor and makes sure I'm steady before he pushes his hand through his hair and stares down at me as if he hasn't seen me in, well, a week.

"How is it possible that you got more beautiful?" he asks, making me blush and roll my eyes at once.

"You're a charmer."

"A charmer with food." He holds up a white paper bag, and I immediately salivate.

"Is that Shake Shack?"

"Yeah, sorry it's not fancier, but I was in a hurry to get here."

"Oh my God, I've missed Shake Shack. Not that I ate there often before, because it has a million calories, but we'd always get it on opening night." I take the bag and lead him through my living room to my kitchen, which is open to the rest of the space. My Manhattan condo isn't huge at only twelve hundred square feet, but in Manhattan terms, it's huge.

"I'd say this is an opening night of sorts. Your place is nice," he says, and watches me retrieve plates. "A condo at the edge of Central Park isn't easy to come by."

"Well, there are plenty for sale," I reply with a smile. "But you'll break the bank buying it. I bought this a couple of years ago. I got it for a steal because it was a foreclosure, and I'd just won the Tony, so I splurged."

"You deserve it," he replies simply.

"I think so. I have two bedrooms, two bathrooms, *and* dining space. Compared to my first studio apartment when I first moved here, this place is a mansion."

"I'm sure." We take our plates to the table and sit. I immediately prop my sock-clad feet in his lap, happy to have him close. "How was your trip?"

"A pain in the ass." I shrug a shoulder and stuff a handful of fries in my mouth and chew thoughtfully, then rub my sore leg. "It sucks when there's a delay and you just want to be somewhere *so badly*."

"I've been there," he replies, and grips my foot in his strong hand, squeezing firmly. "Your leg is sore."

"Long day," I repeat. "It's bound to get sore sometimes. But it's not nearly as bad as it was even two weeks ago."

He nods and takes a bite of his burger, and I stare at the way the muscles flex in his jaw. If you look *sexy* up in the dictionary, Finn's photo will be there.

"How was your day?"

"The longest day of my life," he says. "I didn't think it would ever end. I've been thinking of you all day."

"I like that."

"Do you?"

"Hmm." I nod. "It's good to know that the person you're thinking about is also thinking about you."

"I agree. Did you get everything accomplished today that you wanted to?"

"I did. The house is ready to go for a while, and Tony, the caretaker, has it all under control. He's worked for my dad since I was little, so I trust him, which is nice."

"Tony's great," Finn says with a nod. "Your dad recommended him to me, so I hired him as well. And how does it feel to be home?"

"Better than I thought it would." I look around my condo and out to the lights of the city, along with the noise. "I didn't realize how much I missed the hustle and bustle of the city. Not to mention the shopping. I think I'll have to talk Sasha into a trip to Fifth Avenue this weekend."

"I don't mind shopping myself," he says with a wink, and finishes his burger.

"Really? Because the kind of shopping I'm talking about involves many hours deciding on shoes and handbags and lunch at the new café in Tiffany."

"I haven't been in that café yet," he replies, and I narrow my eyes at him.

"Are you angling for an invitation to go shopping?"

"I must not be doing a good job of it," he says, and then scoots back in his chair and guides me into his lap. He buries his face in my neck and takes a deep breath. "Fuck, you smell good."

"So do you."

"I'd like to go shopping with you this weekend."

"Okay."

He smiles against my skin and drags his hand down my back to my ass.

"As much as I want to carry you to your bedroom and sink inside you for the rest of the night, I have some work to do. Do you mind if we sit on your couch and I work for a bit?"

"Not at all." I stand and clear our dinner dishes away. "The script Jeffrey told us about was waiting for me when I got home, along with the music score, so I'd like to start reading through it."

"Excellent, we can work together," he says, and takes his laptop out of his briefcase, along with a folder, and moves into the living room, sits on the couch, and gets right to work.

"Would you like a bottle of water?"

"Yes, please."

I join him, with waters and my script, and sit next to him. He's immediately drawn into his world of acquisitions and mergers while I open the script from Jeffrey.

This is nice, just being together. No expectations to entertain each other, or go do something. Rather, just living our lives together.

It feels comfortable. Normal.

Domesticated.

I grin as I begin reading and quickly fall into a new world.

SHE'S STUNNING.

I mean, she's my best friend, and I already knew that, but sitting here in the dark watching her act and sing is just always such a joy.

Sasha has her script in hand, only referencing it occasionally, as she and her castmate work through the scene. The director calls out from his seat in the first row, and Sasha follows the direction beautifully.

She and I moved to New York a month apart from each other, and were both backup dancers in the production of *The Lion King*. We became fast friends, and were even roommates for a while. In a business where it's hard to know who to trust, it's great to have a best friend who not only gets it, but also has your back.

She doesn't know I'm here. I'm content to sit and watch for a couple of hours, and when they call for a lunch break, someone whispers in her ear.

"London?" she shrieks, covering her eyes from the lights, trying to see me. "Where the fuck are you?"

I walk down to the stage and grin when she runs down to meet me, wrapping me in the tightest hug on record.

"Oh my God, you're here! You didn't tell me you were coming."

"That's because it's what's called a surprise." She plants a solid kiss on my cheek. "You're not usually this affectionate."

"Shut up, you almost died." She sniffles a bit, then pulls back to see me. "And I haven't seen you since you took off for that island."

"It's off Massachusetts, not Australia," I remind her, and brush a tear off of her cheek. "I wasn't far away."

"It felt far away. I have two hours for lunch. Let's get out of here."

She scoops up her handbag, links her arm in mine, and we march out of the theater.

"What are you hungry for?" she asks.

"I haven't had good pizza in forever."

She stares at me with wide eyes. "Me neither. And I shouldn't have any today."

"Live a little."

"You're such a bad influence."

"Which is code for *Yes, London, I'd love to get pizza*."

"Well, duh."

We giggle as we walk the few blocks to our favorite pizza joint, place our order, and find a booth to settle in.

"I'm *so* glad you're home."

"Me too. I needed to be at the beach to get better. The city was stressing me out."

"I know."

"But now that I feel better, being home is awesome."

The waiter delivers my two slices and her one slice with a side salad.

"I can't believe you're eating pizza."

"I had a burger for dinner last night," I inform her. "And you know what? I might have another one tomorrow."

"I mean, I don't want to sound like a bitch, but *how*? How can you eat like that after you didn't for so long?"

"I don't eat this way all the time," I reply honestly. "I've just missed the food we can get in the city. And before you say it, I know I've gained a little weight."

"Well, you could barely walk for a long time, so that's to be expected," Sasha says logically.

"I'm going back to the gym starting tomorrow. And I'm going to try a dance class too."

"Do you think you'll audition for something?"

I chew my pizza, thinking about the script sitting in my condo.

"Maybe, but not for a while. I'm not in shape for it, and frankly, I don't know if I want to go back to the rigorous lifestyle, Sash."

"Ever?"

"I don't know. I'm not twenty anymore, and working from six in the morning until midnight just doesn't appeal to me the way it once did. My body isn't the same. Yes, I've recovered from the injury, but I just don't know if I want to put myself through it again."

"I know, it's a lot of work. You don't have to tell me."

"I know, and that's why I'm talking about it with you. I've assumed from day one in the hospital that Broadway was over for me."

"Which is silly."

"No. It's not." I shrug. "It's never been about the fame for me. It's the work. But you know what? It's been amazing to take some time off. To sleep in, to eat pizza without beating myself up for it later. I kind of like the new curves. But I can't do that *and* live the lifestyle I have to live to be at the top of my game for the theater."

"So what are you saying?"

"Well, for now, I'm going to live my life and eat pizza. Because life's too short to do otherwise. *And* I saw Jeffrey Cameron a couple of weeks ago."

"In London," she guesses. "I was worried about that trip."

"Why?"

"What do you mean *why*? Because Finn is still sort of a stranger. What if he took you there to kill you and throw you in the Thames?"

"Hi, overreactor," I reply, and roll my eyes. "He's not a stranger to me."

"He's a stranger to *me*. Anyway, what did Jeffrey say?"

I quickly tell her about the movie that Jeffrey wants me to consider, and she's smiling and clapping before I get through the story.

"You're *so* movie-star material."

"That's not what this is about."

"I know, it's the work. But it's *good* work, London. And he's right, this could be the perfect way to get into films. You have the talent and the love for it. It oozes out of your pores."

"Ew."

She rolls her eyes. "And you're right, it wouldn't be as taxing on you physically. There would still be long days, and choreography, but it's different."

"I think I could do it."

"You bet your sweet, naturally skinny ass you could."

I bite my lip. "So, I think I'm going to L.A. in a couple of weeks."

"Atta girl. Now, when do I get to meet Mr. Wonderful?"

Chapter Nine

~Finn~

We're shopping on Fifth Avenue in the heart of Manhattan on a Friday afternoon. People walk briskly past us, traffic is loud and constant, the sun is out, and London was absolutely right.

Shopping with her is no joke.

We've visited Bergdorf Goodman, where she tried on clothes for about an hour before deciding on three things.

Only three things. And she wouldn't let me buy them for her, which didn't please me.

We just left Louis Vuitton, which is three stories of bags, shoes, clothes, and jewelry. Again, she compared and agonized, and then left without anything at all, despite my offer to buy whatever she wanted.

"I'd like to go into Chanel," she says, and points to the building ahead.

"Of course," I reply, and guide her across the street, my

hand on the small of her back. Once inside, we're greeted by a woman named Alana.

"It's so good to see you, Ms. Watson," she says with a smile.

"Hi, Alana. It's good to be here! What have I missed lately?"

"Just wait until you see this black leather Deauville tote." Alana walks into the back and returns with a large black handbag, Chanel written in silver grommets on the side. "Isn't it just divine?"

"Oh, I do love this. And you know me, I enjoy a tote." She props it on her shoulder and stares at herself in the mirror. "But this one is a little big. It makes me look tiny."

"You *are* tiny," I remind her, but then hold my hands up in surrender when she just narrows her eyes at me. "I like it."

"We have it in a smaller size," Alana says helpfully, and pulls it out of a black protective bag. "Is this better?"

"Oh, it is. I like it a lot." London sets it down and bites her lip as she stares at it. "I've also been looking for something in pink."

Alana shows her several options in different shades of pink, and London sets them all, including the smaller black tote, out before her and purses her lips, as if she's giving this great deliberation.

"I'll buy them all for you," I offer. There's no need for her to have to choose.

"Right." She laughs, but I shake my head.

"Seriously. You don't have to choose, just take them all."

"That's not how this works," she says with a frown. "What's

the fun in shopping if you're just going to buy everything? I have to consider each one, weigh the pros and cons, and then narrow it down."

I look over at Alana. "When she narrows it down, I'll purchase whatever she wants."

"No, he won't." That frown is still on London's gorgeous face. "Can I speak with you privately, please?"

"Of course." We walk away and she turns to me, clearly unhappy.

"I don't need you to buy me all of the bags. Or shoes. Or *anything*."

"I know you don't need me to. I want to."

She shakes her head. "You don't get it. I didn't ask you to come shopping with me so you could buy everything I want. I just wanted you to join me because it's *fun*."

"And it's fun for me to buy you things."

"Listen to me." She steps closer to me and takes my hand in hers, her blue eyes almost pleading with me. "Please don't do this."

"Okay." I hold my hands up in surrender. "I won't buy you anything."

I don't understand her at all. Don't most women *want* you to buy them beautiful things?

"I'm not going to take anything today," London tells Alana, whose face falls in disappointment. "But I'll be back soon when I make a decision."

We walk out of the store and across the street to Tiffany.

"I'm ready for some lunch," she says. "And I'd like to try this new café."

"Sounds fine to me."

We're seated, and I have to admit the space is beautiful. The furniture and walls are done in the signature Tiffany blue, with accents of the same color throughout the room.

"This is gorgeous," London says. "They did a beautiful job."

We're served quickly and efficiently, and the food is delicious.

"Have you made any decisions?" I ask her as we walk out of Tiffany, our stomachs full.

"There are several things that I'll go back for," she says, and I notice right away that she's slightly limping.

"You've been on your feet too long."

"What?" She glances up at me, and then shakes her head. "No, I'm fine."

"London, you're limping. You're not fine."

"I am," she insists. "I'm perfectly capable of finishing the day."

"Why?" I stop in the middle of the sidewalk and take her shoulders in my hands, making her look up at me. "Why would you do that? We live in this city, London. We can go shopping anytime we want."

"I don't want to go another day, I want to go *today*." She thrusts her chin in the air and glares at me.

Rather than reply, I pull my cell phone out and call my driver, telling him to pick us up on the corner of Fifth and Fifty-Sixth.

"Didn't you hear me?" she demands. I see our car turn the corner, coming toward us, and I lean in to press my lips against London's ear.

"I heard you, but you're acting like a spoiled brat, and I need to get you in the back of that limo so no one can see me when I spank your ass."

She gasps and looks up at me in shock when the car comes to a stop at the curb. I hold the door open for her, and once we're settled inside, I close the partition between us and the driver, and confident that the tinted windows conceal us from anyone outside of the car, I do exactly what I threatened on the sidewalk.

I turn her away from me and land a swat on her perfect little ass.

"What the fuck, Finn?"

"Next time you won't have pants on."

"You don't get to just *spank* me."

"And you don't get to wear yourself out to the point of *limping* just because you're fucking stubborn. You're hurting yourself for no reason, and I won't have it. I'll put up with a lot, but I won't have you hurt."

She seems to lose her fire for a moment, processing my words.

"I'm a grown woman," she says.

"Don't I know it," I reply. "I can't keep my fucking hands off you, sweetheart."

"Well, you're keeping them off me now," she points out. "You're over there with your arms crossed."

"Because I don't want to be gentle with you right now."

"I'm not feeling particularly gentle myself."

I can't take it anymore. Her fire-filled eyes and sassy mouth are too much. I reach for her, pulling her into my lap and holding her face still while I kiss the fuck out of her. She's gripping on to my shoulders, taking everything I'm giving her and tossing it right back to me.

"Get your pants off," I growl, and she doesn't miss a beat. She slips off my lap, shimmies out of the tight jeans and her panties, and then straddles me. "And if you think you're controlling even one second of this, you have another think coming."

"Prove it," she says, panting hard. She's thrown down the gauntlet and I intend not only to take it, but to destroy it.

I quickly turn us so her ass is on the seat, pull it to the edge, and spread her legs wide, diving down to devour her. She cries out and grips on to my hair, but I pull away.

"Put your hands over your head."

She immediately does as she's told, and I reward her by slipping two fingers inside her and pressing my tongue to her hard clit, making her squirm.

"If you move your hands, this stops."

"Bossy."

I grin and pull my fingers out, lick them clean, then suck her lips into my mouth and make her crazy. Her hips are bucking, her back is arching, but her hands haven't moved.

"Good girl."

I back away and flip her over, mindful of her leg, bend her over the seat, and with my lips pressed to her ear, I slide inside her, making us both sigh in pleasure.

But this isn't the time for easy, or sighs of pleasure.

I want her to fucking scream.

I pound her hard, loving the sound of flesh hitting flesh. I raise a hand and slap her ass, not enough to make it pink, but hard enough to get her attention.

She glances back at me, her eyes wide and glassy and her mouth open in silent ecstasy. She reaches back for my hip, but I take her wrist in my hand and pin it to her back, using it as leverage as I thrust, harder and harder, until I feel her muscles begin to twitch and milk my pulsing dick.

"Take it," I growl. "Take that orgasm, London."

She shakes her head, but breathes out, "Oh yes. Fuck." And with her face tucked in her free arm, she comes magnificently, crying out and pushing back on me, until I have no choice but to follow her over.

"We've reached your building, sir."

"I forgot he was here," she mumbles, still bent over the seat.

I push the button for the intercom. "Drive around the block twice, please."

"Yes, sir."

"That should give us time to get it together," I say to London as I pull her back into my arms. "Are you always so infuriating?"

"I just wanted to shop," she murmurs. "But if it leads to this, then yes. I'm infuriating every day."

WE SPENT THE rest of the afternoon, naked, in my bed watching movies on cable. I wanted her off that leg, and naked.

I got what I wanted.

She's been quiet, but I assume that's because she hasn't felt well.

"Are you sure you don't want something for your leg?" I ask for the sixth time.

"I don't need it," she insists.

"You're stubborn."

"Hi, pot, I'm kettle." She scowls at me. "My leg wasn't too bad for me to shop. I would have told you if it was. What am I going to do if it throbs when I'm working, Finn? Tell the director to call it quits for the day?"

"If you can't work, it's okay," I reply without thinking. "I'll take care of you."

She sits and stares at me for a full five seconds, and then buries her face in a pillow and screams.

"I guess that's a no?"

"Oh my God, stop talking." She stands and stomps into the bathroom. She's in there for a long time, and just when I'm about to go in after her, she opens the door and leans on the doorjamb.

"I don't need you to take care of me."

"You don't *need* me to, no."

"But I do need more food."

"How about if I run you a hot bath and I'll order Chinese for when you're done?"

She smiles. "I can live with that."

I walk past her to fill the tub. This is the first time she's been in my home, and I haven't given her the tour yet. I was too eager to get her in my bed.

The tub is tucked behind a curtain, in its own alcove. I start the water, add some oil, light a few candles, and then walk back to the bedroom to find London sitting on the bed, naked from the waist up, waiting for me. She's pulled her hair into a messy knot on the top of her head.

She's fucking breathtaking.

"Ready for me?" she asks.

"Always." I hold my hand out to her and lead her into the bathroom, and she gasps.

"Holy shit, Finn."

"What? What's wrong?"

"This is your *bathtub*?" She immediately covers herself, but I wrap my arms around her and hug her close.

"No one can see you."

"It's floor-to-ceiling windows and it's dark outside."

"They're privacy windows. Trust me, I'm not sharing this amazing body with anyone." I kiss her forehead and lead her to the bathtub.

"This tub is *ridiculous*. It's like a hammock."

She's right. It's supported on either side by a wall, with the spigot also coming out of the wall. But there is nothing beneath the tub except for tile.

"How is it staying off the ground? Doesn't the water make it heavy?"

"Well, I don't have a degree in engineering or physics, but I can assure you that it's sound." She climbs inside and sighs in happiness as she leans back, the water covering her.

"Are you really going to make me take a bath in this beauty by myself? This is a two-person bath."

"If I'm in there with you, I can't order dinner."

"Later." She smiles up at me, and I know I can't resist her. I climb in with her and shut the water off before it flows over the sides. She scoots so her back is resting against my chest and leans her head back. "See? This is nice."

"Very nice," I agree, reaching for the sponge and soap. "I'm going to wash you."

"That sounds lovely."

I brush the sponge over her breasts and her stomach, then follow the path again.

"I should apologize," she says, making me pause. "I *did* sound like a child this afternoon, and it was ridiculous. So I'm sorry."

"Apology accepted," I reply, and kiss her temple.

"I was just so frustrated."

"Okay, talk to me. Tell me why."

She sighs, as if the weight of the world is on her shoulders, and I want nothing more than to ease that burden.

"I come from a wealthy family, Finn. My father, while ensuring that I have a work ethic, indulged me quite a lot while I was growing up. I didn't want for much, and I'm not complaining about that.

"When I moved to New York, I saw so many of my peers struggle to make ends meet while pursuing their dreams.

They'd eat nothing but ramen and scrambled eggs because the rent is so high here.

"I never had that worry. Back when I wasn't making quite enough money to fully support myself, my dad helped me out. I've never had to wonder how I'd balance a budget or worry about the electricity being shut off. I'm a lucky woman.

"However, with that security came strings. He was a good man who loved me and wanted to help me, but because of the help he felt entitled to tell me how to live my life. I was never allowed to make my own life decisions because he held the strings.

"I *do* work very hard. I know that I've inherited a lot of money, but I already had my own money because of that hard work. I've starved myself, and put my body through more than most people can even imagine, just so I would land roles."

She looks up at me.

"As a sidebar, I'd like to clarify that I've never slept with anyone for a role. I won't do that."

"Understood."

No, she wouldn't do that.

"I haven't had to ask my dad for help in more than a decade, and that's unusual for an artist living in Manhattan. I'm proud of it. So, I *enjoy* buying myself beautiful things. I don't need you to buy them for me, and I don't need any of the strings that might come along with them."

"Of course not," I reply with a frown. "I know that you *can* buy it for yourself, but I *want* to buy it for you."

"You're not hearing me," she says, and pulls away, turning to face me in the tub. "That's why I was so frustrated. You're not listening to me."

"You're saying you don't want me to buy you presents. But a few weeks ago you said you enjoy presents."

"Of course I do, but this isn't the same thing, Finn. I don't want you to follow me down Fifth Avenue and scoop up everything I point to just because I say I like it. It makes me uncomfortable, and if that's how it's going to be, I won't ask you to go with me anymore. I'll go alone."

"I'm so confused," I mutter, and rub my wet hands over my face. "No woman I've ever been with would resist me buying them expensive things."

"Then you're either dating the wrong women, or I'm not the woman for you, because that's not what I want," she says, shaking her head adamantly. "If you were to surprise me once in a while with something that we'd seen together that I hadn't already bought, I would think that's sweet. Thoughtful."

"Okay."

"But that's really all I need from you, Finn. When it comes to gifts, anyway. You already do *so much* for me."

"And I feel like I don't do enough," I reply honestly. "I enjoy buying you things. Not because you can't do it yourself, but because I just like it. I don't know if I can change that."

"I guess we'll just have to play it by ear, but what this really boils down to is, I need you to hear me. I know you're not a mind reader, so I'll do my best to be vocal with you when it comes to how I feel. But I need you to meet me halfway and *listen*."

"That's helpful." I smile and lean in to kiss her. "I'm not going to apologize for smacking your ass. You deserved it."

"I can live with that."

"I *will* apologize for not listening."

"Thank you."

"We're learning each other, sweetheart. It's just going to take time."

"I know." She turns back to lean against me. "And we have all the time in the world."

Chapter Ten

~London~

It's two weeks later, and we're on our way to dinner. Finn is driving this evening, and I'm holding on to my new black leather Chanel bag.

That I bought myself, thank you very much.

"So, we're going to dinner with Carter?" I ask, and watch in awe as Finn easily maneuvers his way through traffic. I've never been brave enough to drive in the city.

"Yes, and his date."

"Who's his date?"

"I have no idea," he replies with a laugh. "He called me yesterday and said that he has a first date with a nice woman, but he's not ready to go it alone yet, so I offered to double with him."

"So no one really knows her." I frown. "What if she's horrible?"

"If he asked her out, she's not horrible," Finn says with a laugh.

"True. Okay, well, this should be fun. How much has he dated since your sister died?"

"I believe this is the first," he says.

"Oh, wow." I swallow hard and watch the cars as they go by. "It must be hard to start all over."

"Especially when you have a child," Finn agrees. "I don't think Gabby was ready either."

"Do you think she is now?"

"I doubt it," he says with a shrug. "But what's he supposed to do? Be alone forever?"

"No. It's a tough place to be in."

Finn exits off the freeway and finds the restaurant, leaves his Mercedes with the valet, and escorts me inside.

Carter and his date are already waiting for us, and the look of sheer terror and relief when he sees us is slightly humorous.

"Hey," he says as he stands and shakes Finn's hand. "You must be London."

"It's nice to meet you," I reply, and am surprised to be folded in a big hug. "The Cavanaugh family is a bunch of huggers."

"Guilty," Carter says, and smiles down at me. "Even if my last name is Shaw, the hugging has rubbed off on me."

I turn to see a pretty, petite blonde smiling at us. Her makeup is impeccable, her nails recently done, and she is also carrying a Chanel handbag.

We're going to have plenty to talk about.

"I'm London," I say, holding out my hand.

"Zoe," she replies with a smile, shaking both Finn's hand and mine. We all sit, and I don't give the awkward silence a chance to settle in.

"So, Carter, how did you and Zoe meet?"

"At a coffee shop," she says before he can. "We go to the same one every morning, around the same time. I finally got the nerve up to talk to him about a week ago."

"That's so fun," I reply with a smile. "I don't think I know anyone who's met that way."

Zoe smiles warmly and rubs Carter's arm, which seems to make him uncomfortable. He takes a sip of his water.

Carter is definitely not ready for this, the poor guy. And I feel badly for Zoe because she seems to be really into him.

Ugh.

Finn lays his hand on my thigh under the table and gives it a gentle squeeze. I'm not sure if he's thanking me for spearheading the conversation, but I do my best to keep it going.

"And what do you do, Zoe?"

"I'm a financial adviser," she says. "I do math all day long."

"Well, bless you, because math makes me break out in hives."

"Someone has to do it," Finn says with a smile, and easily steers the conversation to investments and stocks, which I try to keep up with, but my experience with the subject is limited.

Carter also participates and starts to loosen up, and at one point, actually puts his hand on Zoe's shoulder, which I take as a good sign.

"How do you and Finn know each other, Carter?" Zoe asks, and takes a bite of her salad.

"Oh," Carter says, surprised. He's blinking, looking to Finn for help.

"Carter and I are brothers-in-law," Finn replies smoothly. "He was married to my late sister."

"I see."

And just like that, Zoe completely shuts down. I can almost see the brick walls being constructed around her, and her eyes have gone cool.

She sets her napkin on the table and stands. "If you'll excuse me, I'm going to visit the restroom."

She walks away, and the guys both look around, dumbfounded.

"What did I say?" Finn asks.

"It's okay. I'll go talk to her." I pat Finn's arm and then follow Zoe into the women's restroom. We're the only two in there when I arrive, and Zoe is standing at the sink, leaning on the countertop, her head bowed.

"I take it Carter hadn't gotten around to telling you that he'd been married before."

She looks up at me with sad eyes. "No. He hadn't."

"And it looks like that's a problem for you."

She sighs and turns, resting her hips on the countertop now, and crosses her arms over her chest.

"Did he tell you he has a daughter?"

"Yes."

At least he wasn't a douchebag.

"And I don't mean to sound petty," Zoe says, shaking her head. "But I can't compete with a ghost, London. I can accept a child, and if he were divorced, well, it happens all the time.

"But a widower? That's tough because I don't want to feel like I'm being compared to someone who isn't here anymore. And if the way he's acting is any indication, I don't think he's dated much, which only makes it worse."

"I get it," I reply with a nod. "I only just met Carter tonight, so I don't know him, but Finn has always had great things to say about him."

"He seems like a nice guy," Zoe agrees. "That's what sucks so badly. Do you know how hard it is to meet a nice guy in this city?"

"You're preaching to the choir, sister. And for the record, I didn't meet Finn here, I technically met him on Martha's Vineyard."

"Maybe I should move there," she says with a sigh. "Should I just go home?"

"No." I shake my head adamantly and pat her arm. "You're here, and we're nice people. Enjoy your dinner and the conversation, knowing that you don't want anything more than being friendly acquaintances with Carter. That's totally allowed."

"You're right." She nods and checks her hair in the mirror. "Let's go back out there."

"Sorry," I say when we get back to the table. "We got caught up talking about girl stuff. How is Gabby, Carter?"

He smiles, and relaxes a bit more. "She's doing really well, thanks. She talks about you all the time."

"She's a sweet girl."

Carter coughs, almost choking on his wine.

"Don't tell me you don't think she's sweet."

"She's always been sweet," he confirms, and looks to Finn for help.

"She's just been a handful lately," Finn adds.

"Well, I enjoyed her. I'd like to see her again."

Our entrées are delivered, and the rest of dinner seems to be easier. Maybe it's because Zoe has decided that Carter isn't the man for her, I don't know. But the atmosphere is lighter.

After dessert has come and gone, and I'm stuffed to the gills, Finn's phone rings.

"It's Quinn," he says to Carter, who just shrugs. "This is Finn."

He listens for a moment, his eyes narrowing, and I have a very bad feeling.

"Which hospital? Uh-huh. Carter and I just finished dinner. We're not far from there. Yeah, we're on our way."

He hangs up and tucks his phone away, then waves our waitress down.

"What's going on?" Carter asks.

"Mom's in the hospital," Finn says, his voice cold steel.

"What happened?" I ask.

"Quinn didn't give me any specifics, just said we need to get there. I don't know what's happening."

"I'll take Zoe home and meet you there," Carter says, but Zoe shakes her head no.

"I'll grab a cab, Carter." Carter frowns, but Zoe insists. "Really, it's okay. You should go be with your family."

"You're absolutely sure?"

"Yes." She smiles at all of us. "I'm sorry for the way it's ending, but I had a nice evening."

We wait to make sure Zoe is safely in a cab before we leave for the hospital.

"I want to know what's going on," Carter grumbles as he walks to his car.

"Me too," Finn says grimly.

I HATE THE smell of hospitals. Disinfectant that seems to cling to my nostrils. They all smell the same, including this one. We're walking down a long hallway, after a receptionist gave us Maggie's room number.

Carter and Finn are walking like two men on a mission, and I have to practically jog to keep up with them. Their faces are fierce.

I definitely wouldn't want to go up against them in a courtroom.

"I'm telling you, I'm perfectly fine," we hear Maggie yell down the hallway, and I glance up in time to see Finn's lips twitch with humor.

"She's well enough to yell," Carter says, relief in his voice.

We get to the doorway, and both men hurry in. There's a

third man, dressed in an old rock concert T-shirt and worn jeans, sitting in a chair across the room from her.

He looks just like Finn.

I hang back near the door and watch the scene before me. All three men are at the older woman's bedside, and even in her hospital gown, she's clinging on to her handbag, her face in a scowl.

"What's going on, Mom?" Finn asks as he takes her hand in his.

"That fool," she begins, pointing to Quinn, "called the ambulance for me."

"Back up," Carter says. "*Why* did he call the ambulance?"

"Because she passed out," Quinn replies. "She went into the restroom and passed out, fell over, hit her head."

"Mom?" Finn asks.

"I had a headache," she says.

"You could have had a stroke," Quinn says. "She called me, all disoriented, and told me she fell. So naturally I called 911 and hauled ass to her house."

"Watch your language," Maggie snaps. "Yes, I have a headache. And its name is Quinn, you little shit."

"*Did* you have a stroke?" Carter asks.

"No," she says.

"Maybe," Quinn interrupts. "The tests aren't back yet."

"She doesn't seem to have paralysis, slurred speech, or any of the other warning signs," Finn says.

"It could have been a mild stroke," Quinn insists, and then notices me standing here. "Who's this?"

"I'm London," I reply. "Sorry, I was with these two when you called."

"You have nothing to be sorry for," Maggie says, and smiles at me. "I see one of my boys is doing something right. Quinn, take notes."

"Oh, for fucksake," Quinn mutters.

"I said watch your mouth. Hello, London. It's good to see you."

"It's good to see you too, but I wish it wasn't in a hospital."

"Quinn's fault," she says again. "And not only did he call the ambulance, they came barreling down my street with the lights and sirens going. How am I supposed to explain that to the neighbors? It's humiliating, that's what it is."

"No, it isn't," Carter says gently. "We need to make sure that you're okay. You're the only one like you that we have."

"Although, Quinn is a bit paranoid," Finn concedes.

"Making sure my mother didn't have a stroke is paranoid?" Quinn demands. "Besides, I need to be on top of it. People in this family have a habit of not telling us all the full story when it comes to medical issues."

There's an awkward silence, and I make a mental note to ask Finn what Quinn meant later.

"There's no need to go over that again," Maggie says, her voice softer now. "What's done is done, and we can't change it. But you can't coddle me."

"I'm looking out for you," Quinn says, clearly frustrated.

"Next you'll be saying that I shouldn't live on my own anymore and you'll all try to put me in a home or something.

And let me tell you right now, I'm not going to live in any home."

"No home," Finn confirms.

"We can afford a full-time caregiver," Quinn suggests.

"I'm not going to have a stranger living in my house," Maggie says.

"Mom," Finn says with a sigh. "Why don't we back it up again. Why did you pass out?"

"I don't know," she says with a shrug, and examines the handle on her bag.

"What was happening?" Carter asks.

"I just walked into the bathroom, and then I woke up on the floor and called Quinn. Which I now regret."

Quinn covers his face with his hands and rubs hard.

"You said you had a headache?" I ask, and sit at her hip, take her hand in my own, and watch her carefully.

"Oh no, you're starting on me too," she says.

"No, ma'am, I'm just a friend, not your child, so maybe I'm easier to talk to." I give her a wide smile and she laughs for the first time since we got here.

"You might be onto something there. I do like you, London." She pats my hand. "I hope my son plans to hang on to you for a while."

I lean in as if I'm about to tell her a secret. "I plan to hang on to *him* for a while."

"Good." She nods and closes her eyes, as if she's suddenly very tired. "I did have a headache. I've been getting them more often lately."

"And then you went into the restroom?"

"I did. I was looking for some Tylenol. Suddenly the room started to spin, and before I could sit on the toilet seat, I fainted. It was the damnedest thing."

"How long do you think you were out for?"

"Now you sound like the doctor," she says, and pats my hand again. "Not long, dear. My test results should come back soon, and I'll be on my way home. But I would prefer if Finn or Carter give me a ride home because Quinn is on my last nerve. Although, he's lived on my last nerve for about thirty years."

"I'm your favorite," Quinn says with a smile just as the doctor walks into the room.

"Well, look at this party," she says, and opens her laptop. "Mrs. Cavanaugh, I'm happy to report that you did not have a stroke, and your heart is healthy as well."

"I told you," Maggie says.

"However, your blood pressure is elevated, so I'd like you to see your doctor this week to get on medication for that."

"It's elevated because I'm in the hospital."

"That could be," the doctor says with a nod. "So it's a good idea to see your doctor this week, and they will take it again to see if it's back to normal, or if you need that medication."

"She'll go," Quinn says, earning a glare from his mother.

"High blood pressure can cause those headaches, and the wooziness," the doctor continues. "So be sure to do that for me. I'm going to give you something to bring it down temporarily."

"Thank you," Maggie says. "Does this mean I get to go home?"

"I don't see why not. I'm going to order that medicine, and we'll finish pushing these fluids so you're nicely hydrated. That's another thing, be sure to drink lots of water. Being dehydrated can also lead to those headaches."

"I drink plenty of tea."

"No, ma'am," the doctor replies. "You need just plain old water. Add some lemon to it if you like."

And with that, she leaves, and we're left with a moody Maggie.

"I'm seventy-two years old," she says with a scowl. "I think I know what I need."

"You're the most stubborn woman I've ever met," Quinn says.

"I've met another," Finn says, and points at me.

"Me?" I demand.

"Oh yeah. You."

"Pfft. I don't know what you're talking about."

"I really like her, Finn. You hang on to this one."

Finn just smiles at me from across the bed.

"So, what did Quinn mean earlier?" I ask when we're finally on our way back to Finn's place a couple of hours later.

"About the medical issues thing?"

"Yeah."

Finn rubs his fingers over his lips and then switches lanes.

"When my sister got sick, she and Carter kept it to themselves for a while. I know that neither of them thought she would die from the cancer, given her age and her previous health history.

"So, they decided that they'd keep it quiet for a while and let her get some treatments under her belt before they worried the rest of the family. By the time they told us, she only had about a month left to live."

"Oh, that's just horrible, Finn. I'm sorry."

"Yeah, I was very angry with Carter for a long time. As you can see, I wasn't the only one. My dad didn't take it well either, and ended up passing from a heart attack not long after Darcy died. It was a hard time.

"If we'd known that she was sick sooner, we all would have taken more time to be with her, to spend more precious time with her before she left."

"It never would have been enough time," I reply, and lay my hand on his thigh.

"I know," he says softly. "I get that now. And it was important for her to spend time with Gabby and Carter, to have a life with them for as long as she could. Darcy deserved that. But it was rough to find out that she not only had breast cancer, but that she'd already been through treatments that didn't work. To be told, *Hey guys, I have cancer, and we've already tried treatment. I have about three months to live* is quite the shocker."

"They thought she had three months?"

He nods. "But she had one month. We all went to live at my

mom's house so we could be there around the clock and spend as much time with her as we could. I know that wasn't easy for Carter to have to share Darcy with the rest of us. But we loved her too."

"Of course you did. There weren't any other treatments they could try?"

He licks his lips, and his hands tighten on the steering wheel. "There were, but they were expensive, and I *don't* come from a wealthy family."

I stare at him, completely taken aback.

"We weren't poor, but we weren't wealthy. The treatment they suggested was in Europe, and we were ready to sell property, take out loans, whatever we had to do, but there was only a twenty percent chance that it would have worked."

I pat his leg, and he takes my hand in his, then pulls it up to his lips.

"I broke out in my career the following year." He spares me a glance, then returns his attention to the freeway. "A year too late. I couldn't save her. I couldn't help her. And if you think that I don't think about the twenty percent chance that she could still be here, well, you'd be wrong."

"It's not your fault, Finn."

"We all took it hard," he says, not acknowledging my comment, "but Quinn really struggled with it, and still does. Losing Darcy and Dad so close together, Quinn now watches Mom like a hawk. He checks in with her every day, and takes her to the doctor for every little thing."

"No wonder he's on her last nerve."

"She's strong, and she's healthy. We'll get the blood pressure thing straightened out. I know she'll be okay."

"She will be," I agree. "But Quinn's entitled to his feelings, and he loves her. He wants to protect her."

"He's always been very protective of all of us," Finn agrees. "You would have thought that he was the oldest sibling. But it's gotten worse, and he needs to lighten up on Mom. He can't micromanage every day of the poor woman's life."

"He'll figure it out," I reply as he pulls into his underground parking garage. "It was fun to see you all together tonight. Especially after we realized that she's okay."

"Why is that?"

"You're a family," I say, not sure how to explain it. "You joke with each other, and care about each other. I had that with my parents, but not with my brother. So it's interesting to see siblings who get along with each other."

"They drive me nuts, but I love them," Finn says with a nod. "And I'm glad they like you too."

"Yeah?"

"Yeah. Because I plan to hold on to you for a while too. A long while."

"Good to know."

Chapter Eleven

~London~

*S*unday mornings have proven to be my favorite with Finn. It's the one day a week that we sleep late, have lazy sex, and then coffee, breakfast, and more lazy time.

It absolutely does not suck, and I look forward to it every week.

This week is no different.

He's reading articles on his iPad, and I'm watching a cooking show on TV. We're curled up on his bed, our legs tangled, enjoying the quiet.

"I'm totally going to make this for dinner tonight," I announce, already salivating at the thought of the chicken dish that Chef Alex is whipping up on the screen. "It looks easy enough."

Finn looks up from his article to watch with me for a moment. "I think I have most of those ingredients in the kitchen now."

"I'll double-check and go to the store later if I have to. Oh, maybe I should bake banana bread."

"Why?"

"Because it sounds good," I say, and laugh when he just pinches the invisible flab on his belly. "I'm *not* making you fat."

"If you keep whipping up delicious baked goods, you will," he says, and pulls me into his arms for a long kiss. "Besides, this is all the sweetness that I need."

"Aren't you the charming one?"

His hand travels up between my thighs, and his fingertips flirt with my lips, making me squirm.

"Are you trying to talk me into or out of the banana bread?"

"Does it matter?" he asks with a grin. My back is arched, my hard nipples are pressed against the thin cotton of his old T-shirt, and he dips his head to pull one into his mouth, making me moan. His fingers dip into my pussy now and he makes that "come here" motion that makes my eyes cross.

"You're so fucking beautiful," he growls, and brushes his nose over my nipple before pulling it back into his mouth.

"I think you just changed the subject." I swallow hard when he laughs against my breast. "What are we talking about?" Of course, at this very moment, my phone rings. I sigh and check the caller ID. "I have to take it."

"Let's not forget where we were," he says as I press the green button.

"Hello?"

"Hello, darling, how are you?"

"I'm great, Jeffrey. How are you? Are you back in the country?"

"Yes, and let me tell you, it feels damn good."

"Welcome home."

"Thank you. So, I'm calling because I was talking with Gerald yesterday, and he would like to see us in his office on Thursday."

"This Thursday?" I sit up and reach for my planner, flipping it open and staring at the coming week.

"This Thursday, if you can swing it."

"I can swing it. Where am I going?"

"L.A., of course."

"You want me in L.A. by Thursday."

"Yep. We'll do some reading, and go over some of the songs with him. It's really a way for all of us to decide if this is a good fit. If it is, you'll have to come back to L.A. in a few weeks for contracts and such, but I'll let your agent deal with that."

"I've been in touch with her," I reply, still not quite believing that this is happening. "Send me the address and time on Thursday and I'll see you then."

"Fantastic, I can't wait. Safe travels, doll."

And with that, he hangs up and I can just stare at Finn. "This is happening."

"On Thursday, apparently." His lips twitch as he sits up and wraps his arms around me, pulling me in for a hug. "What's wrong?"

"I don't know about this," I reply. "Maybe it's not a good

idea. It's not like I can't find an acting job in New York. I don't *have* to sing and dance."

"Hey London, this is a great opportunity. You should see the way your face lights up when you talk about it. I think you should absolutely go out there and meet with the director and do your reading. If it doesn't feel right, don't do it. But you need to know. If you turn this down, I think you'll regret it. Besides, you've already made it clear that I can't be your sugar daddy."

"You're right." I shrug a shoulder and bury my face in his neck, holding on tight. "This is just so far outside of my comfort zone."

"I can tell. You're not even laughing at my joke."

"It's not a joke. Will you go with me?" I look up at him, and then immediately shake my head. "Never mind. That's ridiculous, you don't need to babysit me."

"It's not ridiculous," he says. "It's not babysitting, it's having someone you trust with you because you're outside of your comfort zone."

"You can say no."

Please don't say no.

"I can absolutely go," he says, and brushes my hair aside, exposing my shoulder. He leans in and presses a kiss to the skin there. "We can stay through the weekend if you like."

"That could be fun. I've actually never been."

"You've never been to L.A.?"

"Nope."

"Well, then we should definitely stay for a couple of days. Feel free to set up several meetings if you like. I'll have enough work to keep me busy while you're working."

"You're wonderful," I murmur, and kiss his chest. "Thank you."

"Are you kidding? I'm banking on you taking me to Disneyland."

I lean back and laugh. "If that's what you want, you got it."

"Right on."

"YOU KNOW I love you," I say to Jeffrey and cross the floor to him, laying my hand on his chest and pleading with my eyes. "You know this isn't the way it looks."

"I don't know what to think, Celeste," he replies, and shoves my hand away.

"Less shoving at her," Gerald says. "You're not just angry, you're hurt."

I put my hand back on his chest. "You know this isn't the way it looks."

"I don't know what to think, Celeste." He takes my hand off him and lowers it, then pulls his hand away.

"Better," Gerald says. "You two do have excellent chemistry together. I've seen your shows."

"You've seen the shows Jeffrey and I did together?"

"Yes, and all of the others. I've seen *all* of your shows," he repeats, and sits on a sofa, as if he just told me he loves cheese.

Gerald has been a Hollywood powerhouse for twenty years. To hear that he's seen my work is beyond humbling.

"I've wanted to work with you for a long time," he continues, "but your agent always told me you were content in theater."

"She didn't tell me that *you* were the interested director," I reply, making a mental note to have a conversation with my agent, Liz.

"Would that have changed your mind?" Gerald asks.

"Honestly, I don't know. Maybe. It's an honor to be considered for this role."

"This role could change your life," he says. I look over to Jeffrey, who just smiles that wide, handsome Cheshire cat smile.

"Like I said, I'm honored to be here. If this is a go for you, and if the contracts work out, I'm in."

"I have to warn you," Gerald says, never looking away from my eyes. "There will be a lot of choreography. This film is a full-fledged musical, similar to *Chicago*, *La La Land*, and *The Greatest Showman* in intensity. You'll be singing and dancing every day. I want to be in the studio a month before we start filming for choreography and to record the music."

"I can do that."

"Are you sure you're healthy enough for the physical demands?"

I lick my lips and hold Gerald's gaze. "I am healthy enough. My physical therapist released me fully, and I can have those records sent to you if you'd like. I've started dance classes again, and I can pick the pace up on that. I've not let up on my vocal training, so that's as strong as it ever was."

"That's good to hear," Gerald replies, and nods. "Very good to hear. Would you mind meeting with the choreographer tomorrow to go through some of the basics?"

"Is my getting the part dependent on this?"

"No." He looks over at Jeffrey, and then back to me. "You've already got the job. I'd just like to take advantage of you being in town."

"I'll squeeze it in," I reply, and stand when he does. "Thank you, Gerald."

"Thank *you*, London. This is going to be a lot of fun."

Jeffrey walks me outside and stands with me while I wait for my car.

"You did so great in there," he says, and pulls me in for a big hug. "Thank you for doing this."

"Are you kidding? Thank *you* for thinking of me for it. We're doing a movie together."

"Yes, we are. How long are you here?"

"Finn and I are here through the weekend."

"So, things are serious with Finn?"

"I'd say they are, yes." I look up at him and then roll my eyes. "Okay, overprotective friend."

"He's not an actor."

"Thank God."

"Nonactors don't get it, London. The fame, the money."

"He has plenty of his own money."

"Okay, the fame, then. It's not easy."

"Well, I guess we'll see what he's made of, then, won't we?"

I shrug and climb into the back of my car, waving at him as we pull away.

The drive to the hotel doesn't take long, and when I walk into the suite, I don't immediately see Finn, making me frown.

He was here working all day. Maybe he went out for something?

I wander through to the master bedroom, and hear the shower in the connected bathroom.

He's in the shower. Naked.

I lick my lips, smile, and proceed to hurry out of my clothes. I stop at the vanity to quickly pile my hair on top of my head, and when I turn to join him, I just pause and stare.

He's so fucking beautiful. That body is sculpted perfectly, the skin is smooth, with a light spattering of hair in all the necessary places. He's not overly hairy.

Thank the good lord.

His dark hair is a bit too long, but I like it, and it seems his brown eyes can sometimes see right through me.

I'm in love with him.

What?

No.

I blink rapidly and watch when he turns to wash his hair. He still hasn't seen me.

I'm in love with him.

And I want him. Right now.

I open the shower door and step inside.

"Sorry, I don't need any housekeeping," he says with a smile, and I immediately reach out and grip his cock firmly.

"Oh, I'm not housekeeping," I reply, and squat so I'm eye level with dick. Before he can rinse his hair, I have the head in my mouth, and I'm giving him the best damn blow job of his life.

"Jesus, London," he growls, leaning on the wall of the shower. I don't care that water is running down his body and onto me. I don't care that my hair is getting wet. All I care about is claiming Finn.

Because he's mine.

Finn urges me to my feet, spins us out of the stream of the shower, and boosts me up against the wall, the cold tile hitting my back.

"You must have had a good meeting," he says, and bites the fleshy part of my shoulder.

"It's been a good few weeks," I reply, my fingers in his wet hair. "I want you, Finn."

"Gathered that," he replies, and slips right inside me. He doesn't pause, he immediately begins to move, and this angle has me about to lose my mind. "You feel so damn good."

"This *always* feels so damn good," I agree, and sigh in pleasure when he licks across my collarbones, then nibbles up my neck. "You're so fucking good with your mouth."

I feel him smile against me.

"I've been thinking about this all morning," he murmurs. "You, your tight little body, the sound you make when I'm inside you."

"Can't help it."

I can't catch my breath.

"Look at me." His voice is hard, and I immediately open my eyes to find his brown ones searing into me. "You're mine, do you understand?"

I blink and nod, surprised by the intensity that's coming off of him in waves.

"This." He pushes into me, hard. "This is mine."

I nod again.

"I want to hear you say it." His lips are almost pressed to mine. His body is doing delicious things to me, and I'm on the edge of losing control.

"I'm all yours, Finn," I reply, and wrap my arms around his neck, holding on for dear life as he kisses the fuck out of me. He's pushing harder, faster, and when he groans in my ear, that's it for me.

He comes right after me, and we stay here for a moment, both panting. I'm not sure I could stand if I had to.

If I'm not mistaken, Finn Cavanaugh just *claimed* me. And it was the hottest moment of my life.

His face is buried in my neck, and when his breathing has slowed, he gently lowers me to the floor.

"Are you okay?" he asks.

"Oh, I think I'm better than okay. I might be bordering on fabulous."

He smiles and kisses my forehead. "You make me lose myself, London. It's new."

I think I lost myself that first morning on the beach.

Could it have been then? I've never believed in love at first sight, but since I met Finn, I've hardly been able to see much of anything else.

"You get washed up, and then come tell me all about your meeting."

He steps out of the shower, reaches for a towel, and disappears into the bedroom. It doesn't take me long to freshen up and join him.

"So, what happened?"

"First, we sang. I'm happy to report that my voice is as strong as ever."

"Of course it is," he says, and pulls a T-shirt over his head.

"Then we ran some lines, and Gerald even did some directing. The chemistry with Jeffrey is still there in spades." Finn's eyes narrow. "Finn, he's gay. And a good friend."

"He's a red-blooded man, London."

"A *gay* one. He's more interested sexually in you than he is me."

His eyes widen now, and I just laugh and walk to him so I can hug him hard.

"And then what happened?"

"We talked. The job is mine, if I want it. Of course I'll have my agent look at the contract and the terms, but if it's all agreeable, it's mine."

"You look hesitant."

I sigh and walk over to the sliding glass door to look out at the city.

"Part of me *is* hesitant."

"London, you're an amazing actress."

"I know." I turn back to him and smile. "That's not it. I know I'm good, and I know I can do this. A few months ago I wouldn't have been so sure, but I am now."

"What is it, then?"

"I'm an East Coast girl," I begin. "I don't know if I want to spend so much time in California."

"It's just for a few months, right?"

"Probably three to four months with rehearsals, recordings, and filming."

"Okay." He frowns. "That's not really that long."

"It's a long time to be without you," I blurt out, and then feel my cheeks flush. "This thing between us is still new, and I don't know that I want to be away from you for months."

His eyes soften as he watches me from across the room. "Sweetheart, I can come to L.A. Probably not full-time, but at least half of the week. And I know they'll give you some days off. You can always come to New York."

"You'd do that?"

"Well, I don't love the thought of being without you for months either. And as quickly as three months can pass, it's just too long to go without being with you. So, I don't really see an alternative."

"That's a lot to ask," I reply, and shake my head.

"London," he says, interrupting me. "It's just what people who love each other do, right?"

"I—" I stare at him, not entirely sure I just heard him right. "Yeah, I suppose so."

"Okay, then. We'll make it work. I'm not worried about that part at all. It's an amazing opportunity for you, and you should go for it."

"It's going to be unlike anything I've ever done before. I know live theater inside out, but I've never done anything like this before."

"You're a smart woman. I have no doubt you'll do great."

He walks to me and lowers his lips to mine. How did this man come to be in my life?

Chapter Twelve

~London~

Girl, you killed it," Sasha says as we leave our first class of the day. It was a contemporary dance class, and it put us through the paces. "Your leg seems to be doing well."

"It's good," I reply, and wipe the sweat off my face. "It's twingy today, but not achy, which is a huge improvement."

"Are you sure you should do the next class?"

"Yeah, I can modify it if I need to, but I think I just need to stretch it out a bit." I drop my gym bag and water bottle to the floor and lift my leg against the wall to stretch it out. There's a bit of a pull, but no pain. The pull is to be expected because I'm still getting back into dancing shape. "I had no idea it was this hard to get back into shape."

"Did you think it just happened overnight?"

"I've danced since I was little," I remind her. "So I've never *not* been in shape."

"You're the kind of girl the rest of us hate." She takes a drink of water and wipes off her own face. "I wish I was naturally athletic. If I don't go to class every day, I'm doughy in no time. And then it takes twice as long to not look like the Stay Puft Marshmallow Man."

"That's not what you look like."

"Yeah, because I go to class every day and I eat celery at every meal," she replies. "Seriously, though, I love how healthy you look."

"Thanks." I grin as my phone rings, and I yank it out of my bag, hoping it's Finn.

But it's not.

"Unknown caller," I murmur, and hit the green button. "Hello?"

"Hey London Bridge," Kyle says, his voice happy and, dare I say, sober.

"Hi, Kyle."

"How are you?" he asks, and I frown, staring at Sasha. She asks who it is and I mouth *Kyle.*

"I'm good. You just caught me. I'm in between dance classes."

"You're dancing again? That's great. You must be feeling better."

I pull the phone away from my ear and stare at it in confusion and then say, "I am feeling better, thanks."

"Good. I'm glad to hear that." He sniffs loudly, which tips me off to the fact that he's probably *not* sober, but doing his best to sound like it. "I have some good news too."

"Oh? What's that?"

"I'm going to rehab," he says, and I just sit on the floor, pull my knees up to my chest, and hang my head in my hand.

I've heard this a thousand times.

"Really? Where are you going?"

"At a place in North Carolina," he says. "Right on the beach, so I'll have a good view while I'm hating life."

"A good view is nice. So, did you get the trust to approve it?"

He's quiet for a moment, and I know I've said the wrong thing.

"Of course I did," he says, his voice harder now. "Do you think I can afford rehab on my own?"

"No, that's why I asked."

"I don't understand," he says, tears in his voice now, and I just roll my eyes. "I just don't understand why you always think the worst of me. Of course I got it approved by the trust. Are you worried that I'm going to cut into your money?"

"Good God, Kyle. Of course not, that's *your* money. It was just a question."

"I'm sorry," he says, sniffling more. "I know you just have questions. Yeah, I would have questions too."

Sasha taps on her wrist, signaling that the next class is going to start soon, and I nod.

"I'm really glad that you're getting help. I hope that it's successful."

"It will be," he says confidently. "I promise. I'm not going to let you down this time. I'm all you have, and I'm going to be here for you."

Right.

"I hope so, Kyle. Keep me posted on your progress, will you?"

"Do you really want me to?"

"Of course." I stand and reach for my stuff. "But I have to go to my next class now."

"Yeah, you go to class." He sniffs again. "I just needed to talk to you, but I guess you're too busy for me."

I roll my eyes again and sigh. "Kyle, this is work. You know that."

"And I can't keep a job because I'm a loser junkie. Yeah, I know. You go to class."

He hangs up in my ear and I toss my phone in my bag and stare at Sasha in bewilderment.

"So that went well?"

"Not really." I shrug a shoulder. "He's paranoid, and his moods are all over the place, which is typical for an addict. But he says he's going to rehab."

"Do you think he will?"

"No."

"Speaking of rehab," Sasha says, "do you remember Fiona Masterson?"

I frown. "The playwright?"

"Yes, that's the one. Rumor has it that she has a new musical that she's been shopping around, but no one will touch it."

"Why not?"

Sasha frowns. "Because it's about addiction, overcoming it, and moving on from it."

I lean my ass against the wall and stare at her. "Really? Why doesn't anyone want to fund it?"

"Because it's a tough subject, and a lot of the heavier pieces don't do as well." She shrugs, and my wheels are turning. "I remembered when Kyle called. I don't know if you've ever thought of funding a show, but this might be a good one."

I'd certainly like to talk to Fiona. I clear my throat as we walk into the dance room. "Something to think about for sure. Let's dance."

She squeezes my arm and takes her place next to me, and my mind drifts to my brother.

I don't believe Kyle's really going to get clean, nor do I think he wants to. He's trying to manipulate me, but for what this time, I'm not sure.

That's a lie. I know. He wants money. He always just wants money.

I wish I could trust that he was being honest. I wish that with all my heart. I don't want to have to bury my brother. But this is Kyle we're talking about, and that's not the case. He's done this to me and my parents *so many* times.

So, no more answering unknown caller calls. I don't have room in my life for toxicity, and Kyle is the most toxic person I know.

I'VE BEEN THROUGH three dance classes today, and I'm not limping. That's a win in my book.

As soon as I get back to my condo, I call Finn's cell. He's out of town for a couple of days, but I'd like to hear his voice.

"Hey baby," he says, but I can tell he's in a hurry.

"Hi," I reply, and hold the phone closer to my ear. "Are you busy?"

"I'm trying to stay busy so I can wrap this up quickly and get home to you," he says, making me smile. "Are you okay?"

"Yeah, I was just wondering if you'd look into something for me regarding my dad's estate."

"Of course. What's up?"

"I got a call from Kyle this morning. He says he put in a request with the trust for rehab, and I just want to find out if that's true."

"I'll make some calls and let you know."

"No huge rush, I know you're busy. But yeah, when you have time, I'd appreciate it."

"No problem. Are you okay after that call?"

"It was weird," I reply honestly, and rub my hand over my face. "But I'm fine."

"What are your plans for tonight?"

"I think I'm going to have Sasha over for dinner, and then early to bed. I have an early class tomorrow."

"Okay, baby. I'll call you when I'm finished with meetings this evening."

"Sounds good. Talk to you later."

"Later."

I hang up and walk into the bathroom, start the shower, and then send Sasha a text.

> Wanna come over for dinner in a couple of hours? I'll
> make you fish tacos.

I step under the hot stream? and tip my head back to wet my hair. Sasha replies right away.

Hell yes. I'll bring the tequila.

I snort out a laugh. See you soon.

"SO WHERE IS Finn again?" Sasha asks a few hours later as we devour our fish tacos.

"Miami," I reply. "Something for work. And it sucks because he comes home tomorrow and then I leave the next day for L.A., so I only get to see him for a little bit."

"That's kind of sweet and pathetic, all at the same time."

I laugh and pour us each our second shot of tequila. I reach for a slice of lime, sprinkle salt on my hand, lick it and take the shot, then shove the lime in my mouth and wince.

"It's so bad that it's good." I smack my lips together and then take another bite of my taco. "And for the record, these are fairly healthy. I only put a little cheese on them."

"And they're delicious. I need to learn to cook like this." She takes a bite. "I still haven't met him, by the way."

"Finn?"

"No, Santa Claus. Of course Finn."

"I know, I'm sorry. Our schedules are all wonky. We'll set up a time, I promise."

"Did you just say *wonky*?" She covers her mouth with her hand and snorts. "Wonky."

"How are we buzzed after two shots?"

"Because we're little and we don't drink much," she says. "But I don't care. We haven't done this in forever."

"Because tequila has a lot of calories," I remind her.

"Stop taking away the fun in this," she says with a frown, and holds her shot glass out for more. "I'll take an extra class this week."

"Good idea." We clink our glasses together and drink the shot. "So, speaking of love lives, how's yours going?"

"I don't have a love life," she replies, frowning. "I have a work life. And a fuck life."

I snort. "A fuck life can be fun, as long as you're being careful."

"Yes, Mom, I'm being careful."

"*I'm* the mom? You're the one who called me every single day after the fire to make sure I was taking it easy and doing what the doctor told me to."

"So we're both moms," she says with a shrug. "And yes, I'm careful. I'm on the pill *and* I make everyone suit up. Safety first."

"Cheers to that," I say, and we take another shot. "Do I know the fuck life?"

"Probably. Jeremy Coolidge." I feel my eyes go wide. "What? If you tell me you've also fucked him, I might get creeped out."

"No, I never fucked him, I just didn't think he was your type."

"He's not." She picks at her taco. "I mean, he is physically my type. He's hot."

"He has a good body," I concede. "And his face isn't bad."

"It's usually dark, so his face doesn't concern me. And yes, he has an ego the size of Manhattan, but I don't have to like him. I just have to like the sex."

"Is it bad that I think that's kind of sad?"

"It's not sad. It's me getting laid on a semiregular basis. I don't have time for a relationship, Lon. You know that."

"Yeah, it's rough to have a relationship in this business."

"Exactly. And this way we both know the score. And the score is, we both score."

Sasha and I snort with laughter, we're snorting a lot tonight, and clink our glasses again.

"Cheers to scoring," I reply, and wiggle my eyebrows. "Scoring regularly is *nice*."

"So Finn's good in bed."

I just nod and take a drink of water. I am *tipsy*.

"Like, porn-star good?"

"How would I know if he's porn-star good?"

"Don't you watch porn?"

I'm laughing so hard now I have to put the water down or I'll spill it all over myself. "No, I don't watch porn."

"You're missing out. Okay, how good is he?"

"I don't know if I feel comfortable giving you the details of our sex life. He's not a fuck life for me."

"Don't give me *all* the details. Just a couple of them." She leans in and rests her chin on her fist. "Love sex is much better than fuck sex."

"Yeah," I agree with a thoughtful nod. Man, my head is fuzzy. "Although we still fuck. We do both."

"That's nice."

"Yeah. And he likes to carry me around. Like, boost me up on things and stuff."

"*Hot*," she says, fanning her face.

"Totally hot. And he's really good with his mouth."

"Gotta love a man who's good with his mouth." We clink our glasses and take a shot.

"Cheers to that," I reply, and then giggle. "So yeah, Finn's got skills."

"Good for you," she says with a nod. My house phone rings. "You're fancy, with your house phone."

"I have to have it for the doorman," I reply, and pick up the phone. "Yello."

Sasha snorts, and I put my finger up to my lips, telling her to be quiet, but she doesn't listen.

"Hello, Ms. Watson, Mr. Cavanaugh is here to see you."

"Oh. Send him up." I hang up and turn to Sasha in excitement. "Finn's here!"

"I thought he was in Florida."

"I did too." I sit back on my stool at the kitchen island and shrug. "He must have come home early."

"He missed the fuck life," she says with a wise nod. "And I can't blame him."

"You're silly." But man, I hope that's the case, because I miss him.

Which is silly. He's only been gone for like thirty-six hours.

There's a knock on the door, and I hurry over to answer it.

"Hey!" I throw myself in his arms and hug him tightly. "You're here!"

"I'm here." He leans back so he can look at me and smiles widely. "And you're drunk."

"Tipsy," I correct him. "And I'm so glad you're here because you finally get to meet my BFF, Sasha."

"Well, helloooooo there," she says, looking him up and down. And who can blame her? I mean, look at him.

"Nice to meet you, Sasha."

"I get it now," she says to me with a nod. "And when the salt and pepper starts? Holy fuck."

"Right?"

"I'm missing something," Finn says, but I just shake my head no.

"I should go," Sasha says.

"No, I didn't mean to interrupt your evening," Finn says. "I just got back to town and thought I'd stop and say hi."

"It's okay," Sasha replies, slinging her handbag over her shoulder. "I need to call my fuck life. I don't want to waste this tequila."

She hugs me, and wiggles her fingers good-bye as she walks out the door.

"Please tell me she's taking a cab," Finn says.

"Oh yeah, we don't drive in the city."

He pulls me into his arms and kisses me softly. "You smell like tequila."

"That's because I've been drinking it," I reply, and drag my fingertips down his cheek. "We don't do this often, but tonight it felt good."

"I'm glad."

"That I don't do it often, or that it felt good?"

"Both." He kisses my forehead, and even that makes my girl parts tingle.

I giggle.

"What?" he asks.

"You make my girl parts tingle," I whisper.

"Is that right?"

"You've been making my girl parts tingle for some time now." He picks me up, and I wrap my legs around his waist as he carries me into my bedroom and drops me on the bed. "And I like it when you carry me."

"I know." He takes off his suit jacket and lays it on the chair in the corner. "What else do you like?"

"I like how professional you look in a suit."

His lips twitch, and I want to bite him. Just because.

"Well, that's good, because I wear them a lot." He takes off his tie and then unbuttons his shirt and they join the suit jacket.

"I also like the way you look when you're not wearing a suit."

He laughs now and steps out of his pants and drops his underwear and he's standing before me gloriously naked.

And turned on.

"That might have been the sexiest striptease I've ever seen."

"I bet you can do better," he replies, his brown eyes shining with fun and lust, and I decide to take that bet.

I climb off the bed, push him to sit on the edge of it, and walk a few steps away from him, my back to him. I cock one hip out to the side, my legs spread wide, and cross my arms so I can grip the hem of my shirt and pull it over my head.

I spin to face him and toss it in his face. I'm just in my bra and shorts now. I do a little dance, moving my hips back and forth, then hook my thumbs in my shorts and turn to the side so he has a profile view of me lowering the shorts slowly down my legs.

I'm bent all the way over now. I glance his way and bite my lip when I see that he's stroking himself, not shy in the least about pleasuring himself at the sight of me.

That's fucking hot.

I stand and turn my back to him again and reach behind me to unfasten my bra, let it slide down my arms, and when I turn, my arms are covering my breasts, holding the open bra in place.

"Let it go," he commands, his voice gruff.

"You're not in charge of this striptease," I reply, and make a *tsk tsk* noise. He raises a brow, but he's smiling, enjoying the show.

Turning my back again, I let the bra fall and loop my thumbs into my bikini panties, and with Finn staring right at my ass, I pull them down my legs, and like I did with the shorts, I bend completely over, giving him a prime view of the goods.

I hear him gasp, and before I can turn around, he's behind me, one hand on my ass, and one gliding down the length of my spine.

"Do you have any idea how fucking gorgeous you are?" he asks. His hand slides down the crack of my ass, over my anus, and to my wet pussy, where his fingers tickle and rub before he slides a finger inside me.

"Oh, fuck," I mutter. I'm dizzy and so damn turned on I don't know what to do with myself.

And I don't have to know because Finn guides me to the bed, but doesn't have me lie on my back. No, he keeps me bent over and falls to his knees so he can drive me absolutely insane with his talented mouth.

I have to grip on to the covers, bury my face in the bed, and cry out as he makes me come, not just once, but twice.

Finally, he stands and replaces his talented mouth with his talented cock.

Thank the good lord.

"I can't stay away from you," he says as he grips on to my shoulders and fucks me hard from behind. "I came home early because I need you, and that hasn't happened to me before, London."

"So glad it happened," I pant, and reach under me so I can touch his balls as he thrusts in and out. He groans, and I feel his balls tighten.

He's close.

I bear down, squeezing around him, fondling him, and smile in satisfaction when he groans and pushes fully inside me, grinding as he comes harder than he ever has with me before.

He slaps my ass, something that I've discovered I really love, and we climb up on the bed to collapse in a happy heap.

"So glad it happened," I repeat.

"Did that sober you up any?" he asks.

"Oh yeah. I'm only a little fuzzy now." I roll over to him and take over my favorite spot on his chest. "That might have been the best sort of drunk sex in the history of the world."

"I won't disagree with you."

I kiss his chest. "I'm glad you're here."

"Me too, baby."

Chapter Thirteen

~Finn~

It's quiet at work today. I don't know if it's a full moon, or a new moon, or if Venus is in the house of the rising sun, but I'll take it. London's been gone for roughly twenty-four hours. I've never missed anyone the way I do her.

I'm a lovesick kid for the first time in my life. I always gave my buddies shit for being lovesick, but now I get it.

I open my laptop and start a search for real estate in L.A. just as Quinn and Carter walk into my office like they own the place, because they do, and have a seat.

"What's up, guys?"

"We haven't seen much of you lately," Carter says, and crosses one ankle over the opposite knee.

"So you thought you'd just randomly come in my office?"

"We could do lunch," Quinn says. "What are you looking at over there?"

"Real estate."

"You just bought that condo," Carter replies.

"And I'm keeping it," I say. "But I'm considering something in L.A."

They're quiet, too quiet, so I glance up to find them both staring at me like I've gone off my rocker. "What?"

"You want to move to L.A.?" Quinn asks.

"No, not full-time anyway. But London's going to be working there, and if this film does as well as everyone thinks, she'll be working out there more and more. Having a place would be much better than living out of a hotel room."

"You can rent a house," Carter suggests.

"Real estate isn't a bad investment," Quinn says, and I nod.

"Exactly. It would be an investment property that we use when London's on set."

"*We?*" Carter asks, and leans forward. "Finn, we have a firm to run here."

"And as you know, I can do a lot of the work remotely."

"Not all of it," Carter counters. "We can't just have you jetting off to follow your girlfriend around. I mean, I'm as romantic as the next guy, but this just doesn't make sense."

"Have I let either of you down yet? I spend months away every year; the difference is now I have a woman that I care about with me. There won't be a problem with my work ethic."

"We're not questioning your work ethic," Quinn adds. "But this is a different level of commitment. It's different if she's here, but if you're planning on being gone, even twenty percent of the time, that leaves a lot on us, and I'm not sure I'm okay with that."

"Fuck," I mutter, and rub my fingers over my mouth in frustration. "Are you saying I should be apart from her for months at a time?"

"I'm not suggesting anything." Carter sits back with his hands up in surrender. "I'm just concerned, that's all."

"Well, if this becomes a problem, we will say something," Quinn says, watching me closely. "Whether you like it or not."

"I would expect nothing less. What do you think of this?" I spin the computer so they can see it. "It's in West Beverly Hills."

"Have you talked to her about this?" Carter asks.

"No." I look up and pause. "Maybe I'll surprise her."

"Don't do that," Carter replies, shaking his head. "Women like to pick out their own place. Choosing it for her is a recipe for disaster."

"I agree," Quinn says. "I wouldn't want someone to just choose a house for me. And I know a woman will want to get what she considers to be her style."

"I think that goes for anyone," Carter adds.

"She's under a lot of stress already," I say, sounding reasonable to my own ears. "I can take this off of her plate and just handle it. So all she has to do is take a suitcase and move right in. We're not leaving New York, so we won't have to pack everything we own. I'll buy new stuff."

"You're going to furnish it without letting her do it?" Carter asks. "Are you trying to be single?"

"I'm trying to help her out," I say, getting frustrated now. "Trust me, she would appreciate this."

"Uh-huh. Right. Have you guys discussed your controlling tendencies?" Quinn shakes his head. "Well, the first thing you should do is call a Realtor."

"True. They can narrow it down for me. Maybe we should sell her condo." I rub my chin and look out the window to the city, thinking it over. "That would really make the most sense. I plan on having her move in with me anyway. We don't need two condos in the city."

"Aren't you getting ahead of yourself?" Quinn asks.

"What do you mean?"

"Ask the girl if she wants to move in with you before you decide to list her condo."

"I'm not going to list her condo. It's not in my name." I shake my head and frown. "That's not possible."

"Because if it *was* possible, that's exactly what he would do," Carter says to Quinn, who nods.

"What are you saying?"

"That you're a control freak, and when you get an idea in your head, you go full throttle, without asking others involved if it's something they also want."

I stare at my brother-in-law in confusion. "When have I done that?"

Both of them laugh, and I just close my laptop. "You know what, if you're going to be dicks, you can leave. I don't have time for this."

"Right, because you're planning to sell your girlfriend's house out from under her so you can buy a house in L.A. that she hasn't expressed any interest in wanting."

"That makes me sound like an asshole."

Quinn shrugs and Carter hides a smile behind his hand.

"Fuck both of you."

"All right, all right. This isn't why we came here," Quinn says, laughing and clearly enjoying tormenting me. "We really should go grab a bite."

"Either that, or I'm going to duck out of here for the day. Why is it so quiet?" Carter asks. "And why do I feel like it's the quiet before the storm?"

"Because you always think the worst is going to happen," Quinn reminds him.

"Sure, mister, I'm sure my mom is having a stroke and a heart attack."

"Don't start with me," Quinn says, getting riled up. "I'm not the one who didn't tell me that my sister was dying until it was too late to spend some decent time with her."

"We've been over this," Carter begins, but I cut him off.

"Enough. No lunch today. Both of you go home and do whatever it is you do to let off some steam. This is an old argument that doesn't make any sense now. It's done."

Quinn sighs. "Yeah, I'm going home. Sorry, man."

He stands and leaves, and Carter and I are left staring at each other.

"Are you guys ever going to forgive me?"

"We did a long time ago," I assure him. "Quinn is still working through the grief."

"Yeah, me too," he says with a sad smile. "I never said thanks for going on that first date with me. It didn't occur to me until later that it could have been painful for you."

"It's not. You have to move on with your life, Carter. Darcy would want that."

He just frowns, and then stands. "I'm going home too. Gabby should be home anytime. I'll help her with her homework."

"Have a good day."

He walks out and I open the laptop again. This place in Hollywood looks amazing. I reach for my phone and make a call.

"How ARE you, baby?" I grin and maneuver my way through traffic, happy to finally hear London's voice today.

"I'm good," she says. "I'm sorry I didn't have a chance to call earlier. It's been a busy day."

"It's okay, I understand. How did everything go? Tell me about it."

"The contract signing took forever because I had my agent and an entertainment attorney there. I haven't done that before, but there is more involved here, so we went through page by page."

"How many pages is the contract?"

"Seventy-eight."

"That's a long day," I reply with a laugh. "I'm glad you brought the attorney in."

"My agent suggested it, and I thought it was a good idea. We had a few changes, and I countered for more money, but I know they expected that."

"Of course." I nod and switch lanes. She's so damn intelligent. "Have I told you today how proud I am of you, London?"

"I don't think so." I can hear the smile in her voice, and I want nothing more than to be there with her right now, celebrating properly.

"Well, I am so proud of you. This is a big deal, and that's not lost on me."

"I know, and I appreciate that," she replies. "So, although it was a long day of reading a bunch of legalese that I didn't entirely understand and then having it explained to me, and my brain is about as full as it can be for one day, I can honestly say that it went very well."

"That's good news. What's on deck for tomorrow?"

"I'm meeting with the choreographer and Jeffrey to run some lines together. It's starting to happen quickly now."

"When do you have to be back in L.A. to start production?"

"In three weeks."

"It'll be here before you know it," I reply. "This is exciting, and I'm looking forward to you being home soon."

"Me too. I'm homesick for sure."

"Oh, I have news for you." I pull into my mother's driveway and put the car in park. "I called to check on the trust like you asked, and Kyle did apply for funding for rehab. It sounds like he was honest about that."

"That's really good news."

"I still don't trust him," I add. "Just because he's applied for the funding doesn't mean that he'll actually go."

"I know," she says quietly. "Trust me, no one knows that better than me. I've been through this many times with him. But, he's my brother, Finn. I'll always hope that he's being honest, even when I know he probably isn't."

"As long as you stay on your toes with him, and don't blindly trust him."

"You've known me awhile now. You know that's not how it is with Kyle and me."

"You're right." I nod, even though she can't see me, and drag my hand over my face. "I'm a little protective in this situation."

"And I appreciate it, but I've got this one. Cautious optimism is the name of the game here."

"Okay, babe."

"What are you up to?"

"I just pulled into Mom's driveway. I thought I'd come check on her, spend a little time with her."

"There you go, being a nice guy again," she replies.

"If you call me a mama's boy, I'll never speak to you again."

She laughs. "No, that you're not. Tell her I said hello, and I'll talk to you tomorrow."

"Have a good night, sweetheart."

"You too."

I love you.

But rather than say it, I end the call. I walk into Mom's house.

"Hello?" I call out.

"Finn?" she calls from the kitchen. "Is that you?"

"The one and only," I reply as I join her. She's building a turkey sandwich. "How are you?"

"Oh, I'm fine. I'm grateful that it's you and not your ridiculous brother."

"What has Quinn done now?"

"He calls me no less than five times a day, just to make sure I'm okay. I'm surprised it's not him showing up, because he does that most evenings as well."

"He loves you."

"He's smothering me," she says, and cuts the sandwich in half, then offers me one.

"Thanks." I take it and bite into it, instantly thrown back thirty years in time. "You always made the best turkey sandwiches."

"The trick is to not put too much mustard on them," she says, leading me to the living room, where we both sit down and enjoy our food. "Why aren't you with London tonight?"

"She's in L.A. until Wednesday," I reply. "She had to sign contracts for her next project, and has some other meetings. But I just talked to her, and she said to tell you hi for her."

"I truly like that woman," Mom says with a smile. "She's got a brain in her head, and she doesn't just smile and do your bidding like the other bimbos you've dated."

"I don't think they were bimbos," I reply, but she just shakes her head.

"None of them were wife material. You don't want a woman who's more concerned with the way she looks than she is about having a career. Those girls didn't want a career, they wanted a rich man—*you*—to swoop in and take care of them."

She's not wrong.

"Well, it obviously never worked out with any of them," I say. "And thank God for it, because London is absolutely the woman for me. Like you said, she's intelligent, and funny. She loves an adventure. She's not afraid to call me out on my shit."

"*Finally*, you've fallen in love."

I nod, but don't reply, and Mom narrows her eyes at me.

"You have told her you love her, haven't you?"

"She knows I love her."

"Dear God, how did I manage to raise a couple of idiots?" She shakes her head and looks to the ceiling, as if the answers are written there. "How is she supposed to know? Because she can read your mind?"

"I've mentioned love before."

"But have you said *I love you, London*?"

"No."

"And why not?"

I shift in my chair, uncomfortable with this line of questioning. "That's a good question. She hasn't said it either, you know."

"Youth is wasted on the young," she mutters. "Do you know, my sweet boy, that I would give literally *anything* in this world to be able to tell your father that I love him, even one more time? He was the love of my life, and I waited a long time for him to come into my life. He took his sweet time about it.

"I was almost thirty when I finally met him, and let me tell you, in those days I was well on my way to being a spinster. There are times that I feel like we got cheated out of so much time together because we met so late."

"I didn't realize that."

"True story. And then he was just gone, in the blink of an eye. London is here, Finn, and you love her. So, you have to tell her."

"What if she doesn't feel the same?"

She sits back in her chair and smiles at me, using that smile that women have when the men they're talking to are clueless.

"She does. I know that for sure. I've seen the way she looks at you, dear boy. Women don't look at men like that unless they've already planned the wedding in their head ten different ways."

"Wedding?" I swallow hard and shift in the chair again. "I haven't thought about marriage."

"Yet." She leans forward to catch my gaze with her own. "You haven't thought about it *yet*. But you will, because I didn't raise my boys to carry on with a woman without marrying her."

"This is the twenty-first century," I remind her, but she shakes her head stubbornly.

"I don't care. If you love her, and want to be with her, you'll marry her, and I don't care if you're turning forty soon, you're still my child."

"Yes, ma'am."

She smiles softly. "My baby is about to be forty. How did that happen?"

"Time passes."

"Too quickly. You've done some amazing things with your forty years, Finn."

"Thank you."

"Now it's time to settle down and give me some more grandchildren."

"Are we going to talk about this all night? Because if so, I have other things to do."

"Fine, then." She waves me off. "Are you excited about your party?"

"I'm not sure why I need a party."

"It's a milestone birthday, and it'll be fun to celebrate it. Now, I think I'd like to get out of the house for a few hours."

"Okay." I stand with her and smile down at her when she lifts her handbag. "Where are we going?"

"Take your mother to the movies. Nothing dirty or scary, now."

"I can do that." I lift my arm, inviting her to hold on to it as I escort her out to my car. "This is a fun surprise."

"Life should be full of fun surprises, my boy."

Chapter Fourteen

~London~

I've never been so exhausted in my life. Not physically. I've been so physically exhausted before that I couldn't walk. No, this is a mental exhaustion that's settled around me like fog around the Brooklyn Bridge, and it doesn't feel like it's going to dissipate anytime soon.

Of course, that doesn't mean that I've had a wink of sleep on this flight from L.A. to New York. I mean, that would just be silly. In fact, I've hardly slept at all since I left Finn's condo just over two days ago.

It's ridiculous.

Suddenly I can't sleep when I'm not with Finn? I've been sleeping fine without him for thirty-two years, but now I can't.

Finally, after six hours in the air, we land and I bring my phone to life. I have two texts from Sasha and one from Finn, which I open first.

> I've missed you. Do you mind coming straight to my
> place?

I grin and reply. I'll see you soon. Just landed.

Rather than reply to Sasha's texts, I call her while I wait for my luggage.

"Are you back?"

"Just landed. I'm waiting at baggage claim and then heading over to Finn's. What's up with you?"

"Oh, nothing."

"Sasha, your text said, and I quote, *I need you right now.*"

"Well, I might need advice. About a man."

"Really? Spill it. Who?"

"Fuck life," she says with a sigh, referring to Jeremy. "I know, we said we don't like him, but I might be starting to like him, and he asked me out on a date. Like, a real date, not just a hookup."

"If you like him, you should go."

"It's not that easy," she says, and I can hear the fear in her voice. "The hookups are working for us. No fuss, no muss. And now he wants to complicate it with dating? I mean, why does he have to do that?"

"Because he has feelings?" I suggest, and hear her snort in the phone. "I mean, I know he's a man, and it's a hookup, but you're fucking incredible, Sash. What's not to love?"

"Yes, I'm fabulous. But the point of the hookup is to not have any feelings that aren't centered around an orgasm. I don't have time to mix dating into it."

"Then tell him no." I pull my suitcase off the belt and walk toward the cab line. "Tell him you want to keep things as they are."

"But that makes it awkward," she replies, and then groans. "Why did he have to do this? I don't want to find a new fuck life."

"I think you're overthinking this. Just tell him what you're thinking and go from there."

"Okay. What are you and Finn doing tonight, besides getting naked?"

"I don't know, I'm too tired to make plans, so hopefully we will watch TV and then go to bed."

"God, you sound old."

"I feel old today. I'm tired. I'll tell you all about it later. I have to hail a cab."

"Okay. Talk to you later."

I rattle off Finn's address to the driver and climb in the backseat. It's almost dark now, which surprises me, but then I realize that I just lost three hours with the time change. The drive is uneventful, and quicker than I expect. I pay the driver, and Finn's doorman smiles as he opens the door for me.

"Hello, Miss Watson."

"Hello, Doug. Thanks."

He nods and I walk to the elevator.

I can't wait to crash on Finn's couch.

Or on Finn.

Once on Finn's floor, I knock on his door, and he opens it, as if he was waiting on the other side.

"I missed you," he says, pulling me inside and into his arms. *Thank God.* This is exactly what I needed.

"I missed you too." I bury my nose in his neck and hold on tightly, breathing him in. "You smell good."

"Are you okay?"

"I'm tired." I pull back to look at him. "But I'm much better now that I'm here."

"I'm glad. I have something to show you, if you're up to it."

"Do I have to go very far?"

"No, not very far." He brushes his thumb over the apple of my cheek, and I'm pretty sure I'd go anywhere with him right now.

"Lead the way."

He takes my hand and leads me to the back of his condo, presses a button, and an elevator door opens.

"I've never seen this before."

"This leads to my rooftop," he explains with a smile.

"You have a rooftop? Like, of your own?"

"Yes, I own it," he says, and presses the up button. When the door opens, and he leads me out into the warm night, I stop and stare.

There are lights strung back and forth across the length of the space. Candles are lit, and there are red roses on every surface possible.

"That's a lot of flowers," I murmur, completely shell-shocked.

"I called the florist and asked for roses," he explains, leading me to a seating area in the middle of the space. "When they asked me how many I wanted, I told them to send all of them. I had no idea it was quite this many."

"They smell amazing."

He smiles and guides me down on a plush chair, then sits in the chair next to me.

If he gets on one knee and pulls out a ring, I might throw up. We're not there yet.

He does lift a wrapped box off the table and offer it to me.

"This is for you."

I look at him with so many questions swirling in my head, take the box, and stare down at it.

"This is a lot."

"I missed you," he repeats, and brushes my hair off of my cheek, hooking it behind my ear.

"I guess so." I take a deep breath and unwrap the box, stopping cold at the sight of the signature black Chanel box. "Finn."

"Open it," he urges.

Inside the box is the stunning black handbag I had my eye on several weeks ago when we went shopping together. I had intended to go back for it, but ended up buying something else instead.

This bag is a dream.

"I know you don't need me to buy these things for you," he says, and rubs his hand up and down my back. "I wanted to buy it for you. It's not your birthday, or any holiday. I wanted to get you something that you'd love, because I love *you*, London."

I blink rapidly and stare up at him in surprise. He finally said the words, and he put this gorgeous evening together for me.

"Wow," I say at last, staring at the flowers, the lights above, and this amazing gift in my hands. "Thank you *so much*. It's all amazing."

"And appropriate?"

His lips are twitching in that way they do when he's particularly happy with me, and I can't help but laugh and launch myself into his lap, wrapping my arms around his neck.

"Yes, it's appropriate. You're quite the romantic, Finn Cavanaugh."

"It seems I am. I'm quite surprised myself."

I sigh and let myself enjoy the feel of his arms around me.

"Is something bothering you?" he asks quietly, his lips settled against my hair.

"I'm more exhausted than I expected to be," I admit. "And frankly, it scares me a little. I only had two full days of work, and I can barely keep my eyes open."

"It was a lot of work," he reminds me. "Is your leg okay?"

"It doesn't hurt. It's a mental exhaustion more than anything. Who knew that stepping outside of your comfort zone could wipe you out?"

"Here." He picks me up and carries me to the outdoor sofa. "Lie down. Put your head in my lap."

"I am usually happy to oblige you with a blow job, Finn, but I'm really—"

"Funny," he says, interrupting me. "Just relax, sweetheart."

I happily oblige him, lying on the comfortable sofa and resting my head on his lap. He drags his fingers through my hair, making my eyes drift shut.

"The city is pretty at night," he murmurs.

"Hmm."

"Are your eyes closed?"

"Oh yeah."

He chuckles. "You should sleep, London."

"You went to all of this trouble, and I'm going to sleep through it."

"It'll be here in the morning."

I just can't keep my eyes open. His fingers feel like heaven in my hair, and I'm just so exhausted.

"Didn't sleep without you."

"You didn't sleep well without me?"

I shake my head no.

"That makes two of us, baby."

I STRETCH AND yawn, loving the way the crisp sheets on Finn's bed feel against my naked skin. I haven't opened my eyes yet, but the sun is warm on my face, the bed is comfortable, and I smell bacon.

My eyes fly open.

I smell bacon.

I glance around and frown, then reach over to feel the bed where Finn was. It's cold. He's been up for a while.

I check the time and gasp.

It's after ten in the morning.

I slept straight through from falling asleep on Finn's lap on the roof until now. And I'm *starving*.

I climb out of bed and walk into the bathroom to do my business. There's a white T-shirt of Finn's sitting on the vanity with a note.

This is for you, my love.

The man is seriously sweet.

I pull the shirt on and pad out to the kitchen, rubbing my eyes as I go. I sit down and brace my chin in my hand as I watch a shirtless Finn work around the kitchen.

And what a show it is!

His back is to me. He's moving effortlessly from the stove top to the fridge, chopping vegetables and whisking eggs.

Shirtless.

Did I mention he's not wearing a shirt?

It's something to write home about. His faded blue jeans sit low on his hips, giving me a glimpse of the dimples above his tight ass. His skin is dark and smooth, and his muscles are aplenty.

God bless him.

"Good morning," I say, getting his attention. He turns to smile at me.

"Hey there, sunshine. Do you feel better?"

"Yeah, I slept." I push my hair over my shoulders. "In fact, I slept so hard I don't remember you carrying me down here or getting me naked."

"Really? You don't remember the hot, screaming sex we had at about midnight?"

"Uh, no."

"That's because we didn't have any."

He laughs and pours the eggs into a skillet and begins to scramble them.

"Who brought all of the flowers down?" I lean over and press my nose into a bloom, breathing in their fresh scent."

"I did."

I stand and walk around the island so I can wrap my arms around him from behind and lay my cheek against his back. "You know I love you too, right?"

He turns and smiles at me. "I know."

"I'm sorry I didn't say it last night. I think I was gobsmacked."

"It's okay." He kisses me and boosts me up on the countertop so I'm out of his way. "You were tired and surprised."

"I hope I didn't hurt your feelings."

"You didn't."

"Because I wouldn't ever—"

"London." He comes back to me and leans in to kiss me, long and slow, before just resting his lips against mine. "I'm fine. I'm glad you feel better. And I love you."

"I love you."

He kisses me once more then returns to the task at hand.

"Now, what do you want to do today?"

"The movies might be fun."

He bursts out laughing. "What's up with all of the women in my life wanting to go to the movies all of a sudden?"

"Who else are you taking to the movies? Be very careful with that answer."

He shakes his head. "My mother asked me to take her the other night."

"That's sweet. What did you see?"

"*Deadpool.*"

I stare at him in horror. "You took your *mom* to *Deadpool*?"

"It was that or some scary alien shit, and I knew she'd have none of that. Aside from the language, I think she enjoyed it. She laughed a lot, and she said that Ryan Reynolds is a looker."

"Well, he is."

"Even with the scars?"

"We all know the scars are makeup." I shrug and then laugh when he just stares at me. "What? It's Ryan Reynolds."

"Good to know that you and my mom like the same celebrities. Wait. Does this mean you might work with him one day?"

"He does mostly action and romantic comedy. I'm a musical girl, so probably not."

He hitches a hip against the countertop, pointing a spatula at me. "What if you got a call from your agent that he wants you to read for a part with him?"

"Unlikely."

"Just humor me."

I pop a strawberry in my mouth and think it over. "Well, I'd probably do it."

He frowns.

"Unless you'd rather I didn't. You have seen how in love he is with his wife, right? They have, like, twelve kids. He can't keep his hands off her."

"I know that feeling," Finn replies as he wraps his arms around me and hugs me close. "Can I have a veto in those things?"

"In the jobs I take?" I stare up at him in horror. "Do I get a say in the jobs *you* take?"

"Trust me when I say I don't work with sexy celebrities."

"You get *one* veto."

"Ryan Reynolds," he says with a satisfied smile. "He's the veto."

"You're weird." I laugh and then grab my phone when it rings. "This is Sasha. Hello?"

"I did it," she says.

"What did you do?"

"I went out on a date with him."

"Wait. We just had this conversation yesterday, and you already changed your mind *and* went out with him?"

"He was persuasive."

"So how was it? Did it ruin the fuck life?"

"It didn't suck," she says.

"Be more specific."

"Okay, I had fun. He's way nicer than I thought. It seems like he has an ego the size of Alaska, but really he's just shy."

"That's good, right?"

"Yeah. And then we did the hookup thing after the date, and it didn't ruin it."

"So the sex was still on point?"

Finn glances over, raising a brow, and I throw him a kiss.

"Totally on point," she confirms. "In fact, we're going on a picnic in Central Park today after class."

"I won't be in class today," I warn her. "I'm hanging out with Finn."

"Tell him I said hi."

"I will. And, Sasha, I'm happy for you."

"Thanks."

She hangs up and Finn passes me a plate with an omelet and fresh fruit.

"Yum," I say, and kiss him in thanks.

"What's up with Sasha?"

I give him the rundown from yesterday. "So, it sounds like they've moved past fuck life and into dating material."

"Gotcha." He nods, but then frowns.

"What's wrong?"

"Did you describe us as a fuck life?"

"No. I described us as a love life."

He grins. "Good girl."

Chapter Fifteen

~London~

This line feels weird," I mutter, and highlight it in orange. I write a reminder to talk to Gerald about it when I see him. I've been running lines alone in my condo all morning, trying to memorize them.

It's a slow process.

My phone rings at my elbow, and I answer without looking at it. "Hello."

"Hey there, London Bridge."

"Kyle." I look up and check the time, then rub my eyes. I've been at this for about three hours already. "How are you?"

"I'm doing pretty well," he says, and I'm waiting for the *but*.

But I could use some money.

But I need . . .

But I don't want to check into rehab.

What's it going to be this time?

"But I could use your help."

Here we go.

"What do you need?"

"Well, I'm kind of nervous to check into this place down here in North Carolina. To be honest, it's a scary thing, London."

"I can see that." My voice sounds distant and cold, and part of me hates that, but the other part of me knows that it's just how I have to be where Kyle is concerned.

"It would help so much if you could come down here and be with me when I check in."

I frown and pull the phone away to look at it and then press it back to my ear. "You want me to come there?"

"Yeah, I really do," he says.

"I don't think that's possible, Kyle. I'm gearing up for a new job, and I don't think I can get away to come down there."

"Hey, it's okay," he says. "I know that I'm not your favorite person. But will you please just think about it? It would make it a lot easier for me, not that you owe me anything."

I want to say, *I'm sorry, is this* my *brother?*

But I know that'll just start a fight, so I keep my mouth shut.

"I've been doing a lot of thinking," he continues. "With Mom and Dad gone, you're all I have, and you're my baby sister. I should have done a better job of taking care of you. I'm sorry I haven't been there for you, and I'm especially sorry for the way I acted after they died. You didn't deserve that.

"I love you a lot, and I want us to have a relationship."

"Well, maybe once you're out of rehab, we can work on that."

"Yeah, that's what I want." His voice is full of excitement now, rather than the resentment I'm expecting. "That's all I want, London. It would mean a lot to me if we could have a relationship, and if I have to get through rehab to make that happen, I'm all for it."

"I hope this works for you, Kyle. I mean that."

"Thanks, sis. I'll keep you posted."

He hangs up, and I just sit and stare at my phone in complete shock. If I didn't know better, I'd think that was someone else's brother.

Because it sure as fuck didn't sound like mine.

And suddenly the tears begin, and I can't stop them. How many years have I lived my life wishing that my brother were different? Praying for him to see that the drugs were killing him, and that he would want to get help?

I never dared wish for an apology.

Not to mention, until today, I don't remember Kyle ever telling me that he loved me.

I'm a sobbing mess, letting all of the hurt that I've kept inside for so long come out of me. I wish my parents were still here to see this. They'd be ecstatic.

Maybe I should take some time to go down there with him. I'm sure I could move some things around and make it work.

Finn walks through my door, sees me crying, and immediately runs over, cupping my face in his hands.

"What is it? Are you hurt?"

I shake my head, unable to answer him, and he pulls me

against him, rocking me back and forth for a long few minutes, letting me get it all out.

When I've calmed down, he hands me a tissue.

"What's going on, baby?"

"Kyle called."

"He decided against rehab?"

"No." I shake my head and wipe the tears from my cheeks. "He asked if I could come down with him when he checks in. I told him no, and rather than blow up at me, he said he understands."

"Okay."

"And then he apologized." I begin to cry again. "He said he was sorry for everything, and that he hasn't been a better brother to me. He told me he loves me, and, Finn, he's *never* said that to me."

"Wow," he says with a sigh, and pulls me back against him for a hug. "What did you say?"

"I said that if he completes rehab and gets it together, we might be able to start some kind of relationship."

"Did that make him mad?"

"I thought it would, but no. He said if that's what it takes, he'd make it happen. I'm so afraid to believe him, but I think he really means it this time."

"It sounds like it."

"And just before you arrived, I was thinking that maybe I should shift things around a bit and make the time to go down there. Maybe it would make a difference."

"London," he says, and shakes his head. "I don't think that's a good idea. Let him earn it. Let him complete the program, and then you can pursue it."

"It just sounds so harsh."

"I know. If you really want to go, I'll go with you. But I don't think it's a bad idea to wait it out and see what happens."

"You're right." I sigh and set my soaking tissues aside. "Thanks."

"You scared me," he says. "I walked in and you were a mess, and the first thing that came to mind was that someone was hurt."

"I think I was purging some pent-up emotions."

He smiles and drags his fingers down my cheek, then leans in to kiss me. "You're a beautiful person, London Watson."

"THANKS FOR MEETING with me," Quinn says the next day. We're in Central Park, which is an easy walk from my place.

"No problem." We're walking around the reservoir, through thick trees. If you didn't know better, you'd think you were in the woods. "What's up?"

"Well, I wanted to talk about Finn's party tomorrow night. I know it's not a surprise, but we're going to need him to get there by a certain time. He's not usually late, but it will help if I have you helping make sure he doesn't procrastinate, given how excited he is about the party."

"I think he's going to have a good time," I reply with a laugh. "He just thinks a party is silly."

"Okay, now I'm going to cut to the chase."

I catch my toe on something and trip forward, and Quinn quickly catches me, scooping me up around the waist and righting me.

"Thanks."

"Are you okay?"

"Uh, yeah. Thanks for catching me. It was quite chivalrous of you. You'll make an excellent husband one day."

"Did my mother pay you to say that?"

"No." I laugh again and pat his shoulder. "She's on you about that, is she?"

"Every day of my damn life. And she can harp all she wants, but it isn't going to happen."

"Marriage?"

"No way."

"Why not?"

He glances down at me. "I don't have time for a woman and a family. I work long hours, I take care of Mom, and honestly, I like to play around a bit."

"How old are you?"

"Thirty-eight. Why?"

"Just curious. I guess as long as you're safe, you can do whatever you want."

"Safe is my middle name."

"Quinn Safe Cavanaugh. Has a ring to it."

"Now I know what my brother sees in you. You're a smartass."

"That's not all he sees in me." I wink at him, making him

laugh now. "So why did you really ask to meet me here? We both know you could have told me what time to have him there over e-mail or text."

"You're smart too," he says, and rubs his hand across the back of his neck. "I really want to know what your intentions are with my brother."

I stop walking and prop my hands on my hips.

"You know, if I didn't know better, I'd think you were the older brother. You're so protective."

"It's a valid question," he replies. "My brother is a wealthy, well-known attorney. You're not the first woman to be swept up in all of that."

"Do you really think I'm *swept up* in his money and affluence?"

He shrugs, as if to say, *If the shoe fits.*

"Do you have any idea who I am?" I ask him.

"London Watson. Beyond that, I have no idea."

"You must not go to the theater with your mother," I mutter, and walk up to him so I'm barely a foot away. "I'm London Watson, the Tony Award–winning actress, you nitwit. I've been working in theater for *years*, and I'm about to star in a movie with Jeffrey Cameron."

"The movie star?"

"And stage actor," I add, and thrust my finger in his face. "I'm wealthy without your brother. I might even guess that I'm *wealthier* than your brother. And you know what? I give zero fucks about that. I have a sweet condo in Manhattan, right next to Central Park, as a matter of fact, and a house on Martha's Vineyard worth millions. I know famous people.

"But you know what, Quinn?"

"What's that, London?"

"Your brother is so much more than the dollar signs you seem to associate with him. He's a kind, funny, generous, and loving man."

"I know."

"And he is certainly man enough to know when a woman is with him for the money, and when she's with him because she loves him."

"You're right."

I'm breathing hard, still seeing red.

"That was a shitty thing to do," I say at last.

"Well, you passed that test," he says with a wide smile. "And for the record? I knew who you are. I'm not an idiot."

"You sound like one," I counter, making him toss his head back and laugh like a loon.

"I like you, London."

"You'll grow on me," I reply. "And let me warn you. Accuse me of being a leech one more time, and I'll take your fucking testicles off."

"I like a woman with gumption," he says, but he brushes his hand over his crotch, as if he's protecting himself from a surprise blow.

"I've got more than gumption," I reply easily. "I love your brother, and when someone, even you, talks about him like that, it pisses me off. I have no problem kicking your ass."

"Okay, okay." He holds his hands up in surrender and his face sobers. "I apologize. I admit, I was trying to offend you.

If I didn't offend you, I'd know you were here for the wrong reasons, and no one wants that."

"Has he had a lot of that in his past?" I ask.

"We've all had a few women come and go who were more interested in the name and the money than in us."

"That's not me."

"Point taken." He clears his throat. "I have to say, I've never seen my brother quite like this. I mean, he's looking at more real estate, for God's sake."

"Wait. What?"

"All I'm saying is, he's way into this with you. I don't think there's much that he wouldn't do for you, and it makes me feel better to see that you feel the same way."

I want to ask him more about the real estate comment, but I leave it be for now. Could Finn be looking into a different place in the city? Maybe he wants something bigger? Although that would just be ridiculous, because as far as Manhattan homes go, he's got the cream of the crop.

We finish our walk, and Quinn gives me a one-armed, totally appropriate hug.

"Thanks for the talk," he says.

"I threatened to take your balls off," I say. "I don't think I've ever had anyone thank me for that before."

He shrugs. "You love him. That's all I needed to know."

"You probably could have asked me that over the phone as well."

"This was definitely more fun." He winks and walks away and I begin walking down the street, in the opposite direction of my condo. The city is beautiful in the summer, and it's not too hot out today, so the walk feels nice.

Not to mention, my leg hasn't bothered me in a couple of weeks now, which makes me feel like turning cartwheels.

Not that I will.

I'm restless, and I have another appointment to get to before I see Finn later.

I call Sasha, but it goes to voice mail. She's probably in rehearsal, but I can't help but be disappointed that I can't tell her about today's meeting.

I glance across the street, and would *swear* that I see Kyle. A big truck drives by, blocking my view, and when it's gone, Kyle's not there.

"Don't be stupid," I mutter to myself. "He's in North Carolina. Someone just looked a lot like him."

I shrug and continue down the street to my favorite deli for a sandwich, and for my meeting, which is still a good fifteen minutes away.

I sit outside and enjoy it, watching dance videos on YouTube. Dance videos that I happen to be in, studying my form.

Damn, I was good.

My phone rings, making me grin.

"Hey girlfriend."

"You sound chipper today," Sasha says, breathing hard. "The call must not have been urgent."

"Not at all, I was just wondering if you were busy, which you clearly are."

"Rehearsal," she says. "What are you doing?"

"I met with Finn's brother, Quinn, who wanted to grill me about my intentions with his brother."

"That sounds like fun," she says dryly.

"Actually, I threatened his manhood, and assured him that I'm not with Finn for his money."

"Let's be honest, the money doesn't hurt," Sasha says.

"Shut up, I am *not* with him for his money."

"Okay, what else is up?"

"I'm meeting with Fiona Masterson in just a few minutes." The idea sends butterflies fluttering in my stomach. "I'm going to ask her about the project you told me about."

"That's so amazing, London. Seriously. And we need to get together soon so you can fill me in."

"Well, tomorrow is Finn's birthday, so I'll be with him all day, but after that, I'm flexible."

"Okay, I'll text you and we'll set something up. Good luck with Fiona."

"Thanks."

I end the call and toss my phone in my handbag, then glance up to see a woman with fiery red hair striding purposefully toward me, a smile on her face.

Fiona and I have walked in the same circles for years. We're not strangers.

"London," she says, leaning in for a hug. "It's good to see you. I was excited when I got your call."

"It's good to see you too. Thanks for sending the script over to me. I had a chance to read it on the plane from L.A. the other day."

She sits and fidgets in her seat. "What did you think?"

"I love it," I reply honestly. "It's beautiful. Heartbreaking. Funny. It hit me in all of the feels, and that's not easy."

"Thank you so much."

"And I'd like to fund it."

She stops cold, staring at me. "Excuse me?"

"You heard me."

Her mouth opens and closes in surprise.

"I thought you'd asked to see it because you were interested in the lead part."

I shake my head. "I think it's a story that needs to be told. It's important, and I think people will identify with it." I bite my lip. "I can identify with it."

She tips her head to the side, wanting me to explain more, but I don't. I like Fiona, but she's not my confidante.

"Are you telling me that you want to back the whole show? On your own."

I nod.

"And do you also want to star in it?"

I sit back, considering it. It's a beautiful role. "Honestly, no. I don't have time right now to commit to it, and I think it hits a little too close to home for me. But I know that it'll get cast wonderfully. This show is going to be a success, Fiona."

We stay for another hour, talking about specifics, more contracts, timelines, and then Fiona checks the time and has to run. But we both leave the meeting feeling excited and optimistic.

It feels good to support something that my parents would also be proud of.

I stand and throw my trash away, and when I turn to walk home, a man walks down the intersecting block, and again, I'd swear it's Kyle.

"It's not," I tell myself. "He's just on your brain lately."

I shrug it off and walk home, arriving just before the sun starts to set. I can tell that summer is beginning to wind down because it gets dark earlier every day. But I love fall, with the trees turning color. It's beautiful here then.

But I'll be in L.A. I don't think the trees turn the way they do here. At least it'll be warm.

Maybe I'll rent a place with a pool so I can sit out and take advantage of being in the warm weather later into the year. That'll be awesome.

"Hello, Miss Watson," the doorman says with a smile. "You'll want to check in at the desk. Something arrived for you earlier."

"Thanks," I reply, and walk up to the receptionist at the front desk. "I'm London Watson. Did something come for me?"

"These beauties," she says with a smile, pointing to the huge bouquet of red roses on the desk. "They smell amazing."

"I bet they do," I murmur, and pick them up, surprised by how heavy they are. Once inside my condo, I pull the card out of them and open it.

L—

Just thinking about you today.
Love,
Finn

He might be the sweetest man ever conceived. He's thought-ful, and protective, and those are things that I don't have a lot of experience with. Sometimes I think he oversteps a bit, but I have a feeling that gift giving is his love language.

And who am I to say no?

The flowers are stunning, and they *do* smell divine. They make my place look happy.

I shoot Finn a text to thank him, and then walk into my bathroom to take a shower. I pause in the doorway, frowning.

I don't think I left the blow-dryer on the vanity this morn-ing. In fact, I know I didn't because I didn't wash my hair yet today.

But there it is, on the counter, plugged in.

I shrug and put it away. Maybe Finn used it?

Or maybe I'm going crazy.

I roll my eyes and start the shower, then walk into my closet to find some clean clothes. With the film, my relationship with Finn, and worrying about Kyle, I swear I'm losing my mind sometimes.

Chapter Sixteen

~Finn~

Someone is running their hands all over my sleepy body, making it come awake and want her.

Right now.

I open one eye and smile at the sight of London's dark hair spread over my abdomen. Her white skin against my dark. Her lips pressing to my flesh, leaving openmouthed kisses down my body. Her small hand wraps around my dick, and I can't pretend to be asleep anymore.

I rock my hips as she slowly pumps up and down, making me even harder than before. Her eyes glance up to mine, and she grins, before sinking that sexy-as-fuck mouth over the head of my cock.

Sweet mother of God, she's good with that hot mouth of hers.

"Holy fuck," I growl, shoving my fingers in her hair and

holding on. Her lips pucker, gripping on to my sensitive skin, sucking just hard enough to make my damn eyes cross.

She licks down to my balls, down the crease of my thigh, and then, with the happiest smile on her gorgeous face, climbs over me, and sheathes me in her hot, wet pussy.

"Good morning," she whispers, and leans down to kiss me. "I couldn't wait any longer to wish you happy birthday."

"Best birthday ever."

I grip on to her hips and watch as she moves slowly, rocking back and forth. She plants her hands on my chest, leaning on me. Her breasts are firm and high. Nipples tight.

She bites her lip and lets her hair fall in messy waves.

I've never seen anything so fucking beautiful in all my life.

I start to move now, quickly pushing up, impaling her. She gasps, and opens her eyes to watch me.

"You're amazing," I murmur as I sit up, wrap my arms around her, and hold on tightly. "So damn beautiful."

Her lips find mine, eagerly kissing and biting, loving me with everything in her. It's overwhelming and humbling.

Sexy as I don't know what.

She bears down, squeezing my cock like a vise, and I know that I'm not going to last much longer. She grips my face in her hands and says, "Do it. Come."

I can't help but follow her command, the orgasm moving through me powerfully.

I roll us over, putting London on her back, and lazily kiss her chest, her breasts, her shoulder.

"I love you," I whisper.

"I love you too," she replies with a smile.

My phone begins to ping with text messages, so I roll over and reach for it.

"You let me sleep until nine?"

"It's your birthday," she replies with a shrug. "Everyone should sleep in on their birthday."

I flip the phone to silent and rub my hand over my face. *Forty.*

How the fuck did I get to forty already?

"How are you?" she asks.

"Old." I shake my head and climb out of bed, then saunter around the bed to take her hand and bring her with me. "Your man is old, baby."

"Not *that* old," she says with a laugh. "Where are we going?"

"To choose assisted living housing for me."

"You don't need that." She kisses my shoulder. "I'll take care of you."

I laugh and boost her up onto the bathroom vanity, grinning when she yelps at the cold on her bare ass.

"That's for calling me old."

"*You* called you old," she reminds me, and tugs me closer to stand between her spread thighs. "Besides, you didn't fuck me like you're an old man."

"I made love to you." I plant my hands on either side of her hips and lean in to kiss her. "Like a man who loves you."

"Indeed." She scoots closer, pressing her hot pussy against

my dick, making it start to firm up again. "I don't think you're too old for round two."

"No?"

She shakes her head no and reaches between us to wrap her small hand around me again.

"Feels like this agrees," she whispers.

"You're quite aggressive this morning."

"You're sexy," she murmurs, kissing my chest. "And I want you."

"I'm right here."

She guides me inside her and we both gasp. I just had her not twenty minutes ago, and I want her more than ever.

I look into the mirror, enthralled with the way her back looks as she holds on to me. It flexes, her ass shifts, her hair falls like a curtain down her slim back.

"You're so beautiful."

"Back at you," she breathes. "Jesus, Finn, I'm going to come again."

"Good. Do it." I lick my thumb and press it to her hard clit. "Come apart for me, baby."

She cries out, her pussy pulsing around me and hips pressing hard against me. I lean one hand on the mirror behind her, unable to stay upright on my own, and come hard inside her.

"You make me crazy," I mutter, trying to catch my breath.

"Good." She kisses my chin. "Because you do the same to me. Now we have to take a shower and get dressed because we're headed to breakfast."

"We are?"

She nods happily.

"Where are we going?"

"It's your birthday," she reminds me. "We're going to your favorite spot."

"This birthday thing isn't as bad as I thought it would be."

"Why did you think it would be bad?"

"Did you hear me when I mentioned that I'm old?"

She rolls her eyes and hops down from the vanity, saunters to the shower, and flips it on, letting the water run to warm up.

"You're not old. You're experienced. Life experience is sexy, Finn."

"I have plenty of that," I agree. "Do you plan to take that shower by yourself?"

"Hell no, I plan to bring you with me so I can clean you up."

I cock an eyebrow and cross my arms over my chest, watching her.

"Is that so?"

"Oh, it's so." She returns to me and takes my hand in hers. She kisses it, then pulls me in the direction of the shower. "And you're going to like it."

"I have no doubt."

"I NEED A nap," I say six hours later. We've had a *lot* of sex today. Went out for breakfast and shopping, wandered the city, enjoying each other. I'm exhausted.

"No naps today, old man," she says with a laugh, and I narrow my eyes at her.

"Do I need to remind you just how *old* I am?"

"Hey, you've been calling yourself old all day. You can't sleep. I just remembered that I have to tell you something."

"Okay, shoot."

She grins and her eyes are dancing as she sits up on the bed, facing me. She's excited about something.

"I'm going to fully fund a new show." She talks quickly, explaining that it's a show about addiction, written by someone she's known for a long time. Her passion is palpable. "I know it's going to be amazing, Finn. The script is stellar."

"This is exciting," I reply, nodding. "It sounds like an amazing opportunity if you want to return to the stage."

"Not in this one." She shakes her head. "I can't. It's too close to home."

"I can see that."

"It's honestly enough for me to invest in it."

"I'd like to invest in it as well."

She scowls and sits back. "What? Why?"

"Because it's important to you."

"That's right, it's important to *me*."

I frown back at her. "London, I want to support this with you."

"I need this," she replies, and takes my face in her hands. "I'm not shutting you out, I'm telling you that I need this for me. Without you."

"Feels like you're shutting me out."

"Let me have this," she says. "I don't need you to come save the day."

"Keep telling me you don't need me, sweetheart, and I'll learn to believe it."

She closes her eyes and shakes her head. "That's not what I mean. I don't need your money to help me fund this. Your support, excitement, and love are so huge to me, Finn. *That's* what I need."

"You have it."

She leans in and kisses my jawline. "Thank you. Now, I have to give you something, and then we have to get ready to go to your party."

"I'd rather skip the party."

"No way." She shakes her head adamantly. "Quinn and your mom put a lot of thought and time into planning this."

"Isn't that weird to you? My mommy planned my fortieth birthday?"

"It's sweet." She slaps my arm and I rub the spot, frowning at her.

"Are you always violent?"

She just rolls her eyes and laughs, then disappears in my closet. Seconds later, she returns with a wrapped box in her hands.

"I want to give you your present when we aren't with the others."

"All day today has been a gift," I reply. "I've had a great time."

"Good, that was my goal." She leans in to press her lips to mine sweetly. "But I can't let this day go by without giving the man I love a present. So please open it."

"I wouldn't want to be rude," I reply, and tear into the red-and-black paper. I feel my eyes widen at the red Cartier box inside. "London."

"You're not done."

Inside the leather box is a stunning watch. "This is the Flying Tourbillon."

She nods happily. "I saw you checking it out a couple of times when we were shopping together."

"London." I swallow hard, unsure of what to say. This is a ninety-thousand-dollar watch. "I don't think anyone has ever given me a more perfect, or more expensive, gift."

"It's not about the money," she says with a shrug, and takes it out of the box so she can put it on my wrist. "You've had your eye on it. What do you get for a man who can and does buy himself whatever he wants?"

"A Cartier watch, apparently," I reply, surprised that it fits perfectly.

"I took one of your other watches in so they could match the band size," she explains. "I'm sneaky."

"Yes. You are." When it's fastened, I check the time, and note that we have a little space before we have to leave for the party. "I absolutely love it. Thank you."

"You're welcome."

She wraps her arms around my shoulders and kisses me soundly, running her little pink tongue along the seam of my lips and pressing her body to mine.

Jesus, she makes me crazy.

"Is it inappropriate to ask for a gift?"

She frowns and leans back. "Of course not. What do you need?"

"You." I kiss her forehead. "You, in every sense of the word. I would love it if you'd move in with me here, London."

"Really?" She blinks and looks around the room.

"If you don't like my condo, I'll sell it and buy something else. I don't really care where we live as long as we live together."

She takes a deep breath and slowly lets it out, then looks up at me with serious blue eyes. "This is a big deal."

"The biggest deal of my life."

She nods and looks down at her hand on my chest. I'm usually a patient man, but I want to beg her, to ask her to tell me what's going on in that beautiful head of hers.

But I wait, because I don't want to push her.

Finally, she nods again and smiles up at me.

"Okay."

"Okay?"

"Okay." She lays her cheek against my chest and hugs me tightly around the middle. "I think this might be moving a little fast, but I don't want to say no."

"Thank God, because I don't want you to say no." I urge her chin up so I can see her eyes. "I'd like to put your place on the market soon. And I want to show you something."

"Wait, what?"

"Hold on. Stay here."

I rush into my office and grab the file on my desk, then return to her.

"I want you to see this." I pass her the folder and she opens it, frowning.

"What is this?"

"Properties in L.A. The one on top is my favorite, but there are three to choose from, just in case that one isn't perfect for you."

"We're moving to L.A.?"

"No. Well, not full-time. But we need a home there because you'll be working there."

"Yeah, for a few months. I can rent a house for that time."

"This is only the beginning," I reply, and spread all of the properties out on the bed so she can see them side by side. "Your film career is about to explode, London. I can feel it. And I don't want you to stay in hotels and part-time housing while you're there. Besides, real estate, especially in Southern California, is never a bad investment."

"But." She presses her fingers to her eyes. "What does this have to do with my condo?"

I frown. "Well, nothing, really. I just figured that if you're moving in here, there's no need to have two condos in Manhattan. But if you'd rather keep it and rent it out as an investment property, that's totally fine. You'll make a lot of money on it either way."

"Neither of us needs the money," she whispers, and clenches her eyes shut.

"Why aren't you more excited about this?"

She turns and paces away, crosses her arms over her chest, and then turns back to me.

"So, you did all of this without me."

"Of course." I shrug. "You've been swamped, and I did it so you wouldn't have to worry about it. I'll buy the house, and all you'll have to bring is your toothbrush. Or don't, I'm sure I can find you a new one."

"Of course." She nods and then lets out a humorless laugh. "So let me get this straight. You want me to move in here with you."

"Yes."

"Sell my condo, that I bought after I won my first Tony as a gift to myself, by the way, so you can buy a house in L.A. for a film career that I may or may not have?"

"No. Sell or keep the condo, I don't give a shit. But you *will* live here. And I want to buy the house because you *will* have a film career, and we'll be spending a lot of time in L.A. So we might as well have a house there."

"Of course."

"Which one do you like the best?"

She just stares at me for a full ten seconds.

"London, what's the issue?"

"It's always the same issue," she replies. "You're not considering me. You're not *listening* to me."

"I'm doing nothing but considering you. I'm looking at property in California *for* you." Jesus, I can't do anything right today.

"I didn't ask you to!" Her voice is louder now, and her eyes are pissed, and I have the distinct feeling that I've done something wrong.

"Is this because the house is furnished? Would you rather decorate it yourself?"

"I don't give two fucks about whether the house is furnished or not," she counters, and pushes her hands through her hair with frustration.

"I really don't see what the big deal is."

"Exactly. You don't see. You've made all of these plans, made some pretty huge decisions, without even consulting with me to find out if that's what I want."

"If you don't want to move in with me—"

"For fucksake, Finn, that's not what I said."

I'm so damn lost here.

"Look, if you want to buy property in California, buy it all. I don't care. We aren't married, and it's not my money. Buy Disneyland while you're at it."

We aren't married yet.

Not that right now is the time to propose. She might throw something at me.

"But I don't know that I'm ready to sell my condo."

"Okay, so don't sell it. It's not like one is dependent on the other."

She stops to just stare at me.

"You just don't get it."

"No," I immediately admit. "I don't get it. I thought I was doing a good thing, and now you're pissed, and I don't know what I did wrong."

She sighs and then shrugs. "We should get ready to go."

"No, you need to explain to me what's going on in your head because I'm not leaving this house with you angry like this."

"You make decisions for me," she says. "I don't need you to do that. If I wanted a house in L.A., I'd buy one."

"So I'm a bad guy for wanting to buy you a house?" I stare at her, stunned. "Sweetheart, I don't know any woman who would have been upset at the idea of me buying them a multimillion-dollar house."

"I'm not *any* woman," she reminds me. "We've been through this before. More than once. And if that's what you want, if that's the kind of woman that turns you on, we should end this right here and now. Because that's not me, Finn. I have a voice, and I'll be goddamned if you're not going to listen to it."

"I'm listening to it right now, but it's not making any sense."

"This is impossible."

"No, it's not." I catch her arm when she tries to stomp away.

"You're not listening. You're so damn stubborn that you're not listening to me." She pulls her arm away. "And if we're going to get to this party on time, we need to get ready."

"Fuck the party."

"No." She scowls at me. "We won't blow it off. We're going. You think you can take charge? Well, so can I, and I say we go, make nice all evening, and we will get back to this later. Your mom and brother are good people who love you, and we won't hurt them by not showing up."

"So now you're saying that I'm not a good person."

"I want to stab my own eyes out," she mutters, and presses the heels of her hands against them, rubbing hard. "Just stab them. Maybe I'll stab you first."

"You're not the only stabby one in the room."

"What do you want from me?" London asks.

"I want you to be happy," I reply honestly. "I want you to be as stress-free and happy as possible. I thought I did that for you."

"Most of the time you do. But we are clearly still having a communication breakdown here, Finn. Because you want me to just smile and nod and give you what you want without asking questions, and I can't."

"Well, should I apologize for wanting to make your life easier, London?"

"No." She blinks rapidly and turns away, walking into the bedroom, and I follow her. "I don't want you to apologize for that. There is a long list of other things to apologize for."

"Well, why don't you make me a list, and I'll get to work on that."

She laughs now. Fucking laughs, and I'm so damn frustrated I want to punch a hole in the wall.

There are moments I just can't figure her out. Or women as a species.

They completely baffle me.

"Is this funny?"

"It's laugh or cry right now, Finn, and crying will fuck my face up, so I'm laughing. Because I'm going to wear my sexy dress and look pretty for tonight. I've been looking forward to it. I want to make your tongue hang out and your dick hard."

"You do that without the dress."

"Well, then, just wait until you see me. But if you think you're getting your hands on me before we resolve this, you're very mistaken."

"Now you're withholding sex?"

"I'm going to punch you," she mutters, and slams the closet door.

Chapter Seventeen

~London~

I look fantastic. I bought this red dress a week ago, specifically for this occasion. It's cut low in the front *and* the back, and shows off my legs nicely.

It's essentially a napkin.

Add the fuck-me shoes and my hair piled high on my head, and I'm red-carpet worthy, if I do say so myself.

I walk past a waiter and lift a glass of champagne off his tray and take a sip. It goes down smooth. A few more sips and my ruffled feathers might start to calm down.

Finn is across the room chatting with some friends from law school that came into town for this occasion, as a surprise for him. He's laughing, but his eyes search the rooftop until they find me, and they burn as he takes me in from head to toe.

How can we be completely irritated with each other and still want to fuck each other into next week?

I don't get it.

"You don't look happy," Quinn says as he joins me, sipping his own glass of bubbly.

"I'm great." I offer him a wide smile, but he just cocks an eyebrow and I shrug one shoulder. "Your brother is infuriating."

"Oh yeah. It's one of his main talents."

I chuckle and then sigh deeply. I glance to my left, happy to see that Gabby's here, in a pretty pink dress, talking to Finn and Carter. I'm excited to talk with her.

Then I catch a glimpse of a man as he disappears around a corner, and I scowl.

Could Kyle be *here*?

No. Impossible.

"Are you okay?" Quinn asks. "You look like you've seen a ghost."

"I'm fine." I take a sip of my drink, and then shake my head. "I figured out what you meant the other day when you said Finn is looking at new real estate."

"Uh-oh," he says, and cringes. "So he followed through with it."

"Oh yeah. He did."

"And how did you take it?"

"Not well," I admit. "Has he always been pushy?"

"When it comes to something he wants, yes."

Maggie joins us, holding her own glass of champagne and smiling happily. She's dressed in a beautiful yellow dress and her dark hair is swept up in a dignified chignon.

"Hello, darlings," she says.

"You look beautiful, Maggie." I lean in to press my lips to her cheek.

"Thank you, London. I think this party turned out just right."

I nod and turn to let my eyes scan the room, catching sight of Finn again. He's moved to another group of friends, still talking, but also still facing me. He catches me watching him and offers me a small smile, which I return.

We need to talk, but I can't stay mad forever.

"Your dress is lovely, dear," Maggie says. "If I was your age, I'd kill to pull something like that off."

"It's a birthday gift for Finn," I admit, and watch her brown eyes light up with humor.

"That's a helluva gift," Quinn says.

"See, you need to find a woman like London," Maggie says, and Quinn rolls his eyes. "Don't you roll your eyes at me."

"Yes, ma'am."

"Hey London." Gabby's face is excited as she joins us. "Your dress is so pretty."

"Thank you. So is yours." I hug her tightly. "You've been quite the hostess, talking with everyone."

"It's a fun party," she says with a shrug. "And Grandma says that to be a good hostess, you have to make everyone feel welcome."

"That's my girl," Maggie says, wrapping her arm around Gabby's shoulders.

"Oh, London, you brought the man from the playhouse."

Gabby smiles and I feel everything in me go still. "I thought you said you didn't know him? He's nice. Oh, there's my cousin Josie!" And just like that, she skips away.

My phone rings in my clutch.

"Excuse me." I walk around the corner to the foyer and see Kyle's name on the display. "Hello?"

"London?" he asks, and sniffs. "Is this a bad time?"

Yes. What the fuck is this game you're playing? "No, it's okay. What's wrong?"

"I'm sorry." He sniffs again. "I know you're counting on me this time, but I'm just so scared. I wish you could have come down with me to check in. I just couldn't do it."

"Kyle." I rub my fingertips against my forehead. He has to be here. He has to be the man from the playhouse. That's the only explanation, but I play along. "Take a deep breath. It's okay. I understand feeling scared."

"I knew you would," he says. "I know you've been through hell, and I'm just adding to your stress. I hate that. But I just don't have anyone else."

"I know. Talk to me. What are you afraid of?"

"Failing and disappointing you again."

"I'll only be disappointed if you don't try," I reply. "Just do your best."

"I can't." He starts to cry in earnest now. "I can't go down there."

"Wait." I frown at the first mistake he's made. "If you're not down there, where are you?"

"I'm at your place."

A chill runs through me.

"My place? Like, inside?"

"Yeah, your doorman let me in."

"I'm on my way." I hang up and hurry back to the party to find Finn, but he's nowhere to be found, so I rush over to Quinn. "I have to go to my condo for a minute."

"Okay." He frowns. "Are you okay?"

"I don't know. Where's Finn?"

"I think he just ran to the bathroom. Do you want to wait for him?"

"No." I shake my head and offer him a smile. "I won't be long. Just let him know that I ran home."

He nods and I hurry out, walking to my building, which is only three blocks away. It'll take longer to hail a cab.

Roger the doorman is working today, and smiles when I approach. "Hello, Miss Watson. Your brother is waiting for you inside."

"Yes, I know." He can see that I'm not smiling.

"Do you need me to call for help?"

"I don't know yet."

I hurry past without smiling, and wait impatiently for the elevator. What the fuck is Kyle doing in New York?

Why isn't he in North Carolina?

He was within *inches* of Gabby, and there's no scenario in the world where that's okay.

I open the door to my apartment, and don't see him at first.

But my eyes immediately go to the kitchen island and the floppy-eared bunny from my playhouse that's sitting there.

"Hi," Kyle says as he walks out of my bedroom. He's dressed in a nice white button-down shirt, black slacks, and a red tie.

"I did see you at the party."

"Oh yeah," he says with a smile. "Great little shindig. But I wanted to have a little talk with you while everyone else is busy."

"Okay." I frown. "You're not crying."

He smirks, and then his face crumples and he starts to act. "I'm so sorry, London. I'm sooooo scared." He stops and rolls his eyes. "That whole act was getting old. You're not the only performer in the family, you know."

"I guess not." I clear my throat, and try to think of the nearest weapon. My heels would leave a mark if need be. "Why are you here?"

"Well, if I tell you that, I'll skip all of the good parts, and I don't want to do that." He smiles widely, showing me his teeth. Teeth that used to be rotten.

"So, I guess this means that you won't be going to rehab? That you're not clean?"

"Oh, London. I've been clean for years. This is just who I am." He holds his hands out at his sides and then shrugs.

"What, an asshole?"

"Yeah, that's a good word." He nods happily. "At least, I'm an asshole where *you're* concerned. Because you always got everything you ever wanted, and Dad always treated me like I was an imposition."

You were *an imposition.*

But I don't say it. I want to know where this is going.

"Okay, start from the beginning, then. What's up, Kyle?"

"This is the best story," he says, and does a little dance of excitement. "Okay, first of all, you're supposed to be dead. And the fact that you aren't *really* pisses me off."

I blink at him, not responding.

"I set the fire," he says with pride. "I set the perfect fire, one that looked like a tragic accident, to kill all of you. If you'd have died, I would have inherited everything and be walking on easy street right now.

"But no, you didn't die, did you? Fucking little bitch, you always did screw everything up for me."

"Wait." I shake my head. "You *killed* our parents? For money?"

"Look who's catching up. You're not exactly the smartest girl in the room, are you, honey? Yes. I. Killed. Our. Parents. And I was supposed to kill you too. Who knew you'd be brave and jump out of that fucking window?"

I want to kill him. I want to run at him and tear him apart with my bare hands. But I don't. I stay where I am and listen, because he's going down for all of this if it's the last thing I do.

"You looked completely stoned in Finn's office that day."

"I'd been awake for days, pissed off that you lived. And then when he told me that those two assholes left everything to *you*, I flipped the fuck out."

"Why didn't you just say that you're sober? All it would take is one blood test to confirm, and the money is yours, Kyle."

"Because I shouldn't have to prove dick!" he yells back at me. "It's *mine*. All of it. You have your own goddamn money, you don't need it. And what do you do after the will reading? You go to Martha's Vineyard to live the life of luxury in your fancy house."

"That was *our* house," I remind him, but he just glares at me.

"It's *your* house now because you stole what was rightfully mine. Do you think I haven't been following you? Watching? How do you think I got the stupid bunny? You thought it was the storm that fucked up your stupid playhouse, but it wasn't. It was *me*. I screwed with the battery in the car. I've been following you."

"I knew I saw you."

"Yeah, I got a little sloppy the last few weeks because I wanted you to see me and get scared."

"You don't scare me."

He smirks and pulls a gun out of the back of his pants and points it at me. "I should scare you."

"You wouldn't hurt me." This can't be real.

"Are you fucking deaf? Haven't you been listening to me? I tried to kill you, you idiot."

"I don't believe it." I shake my head, just as my phone rings.

"Throw it to me."

I pull it out of my clutch and see Finn's name on the display.

"I said throw it to me," Kyle says, and I do. "Hello, London can't come to the phone right now. Who am I? Not that it's any of your fucking business, but this is her brother. She's with me. No, I'm not going to let you talk to her."

"Just let me talk to him."

"Nope, not telling you where we are either." He turns away from me, enjoying the way he's taunting Finn over the phone. He's more mentally disturbed than I ever thought. I ease my way to the end table by the couch, which has a pair of scissors sitting on it, and grab them, then inch my way toward Kyle, who's still talking smack to Finn. "I don't know what you want with my bitch of a sister. She's a know-it-all, and she's not that talented. Maybe she's fun in bed? I don't know. It doesn't matter, because I'm about to fucking kill her."

He turns, surprised to see me standing so close to him, and drops the phone.

I punch him in the nose, satisfied with the loud crunch of it breaking, and stick the scissors next to his neck. "Don't fucking move. Finn! Call the cops!"

I can barely hear his voice from the floor. "Quinn did. On our way."

"You're not going to fucking stab me."

"Oh yeah, I am. Just try me."

"You broke my nose."

"Good."

He bends over, pushing his hands against his nose, and when I move to let him, he reaches out to take me down.

But I move quickly, not inhibited by blurry eyes and a bloody nose, and land my elbow against his face again, sending him to the floor, unconscious.

Seconds later, there's pounding on my door, and cops come flooding inside.

"London Watson?"

"Yes. This is Kyle Watson, and I'm pressing charges for breaking and entering, assault, and the murder of my parents."

The lead detective stops and stares at me.

"You heard me correctly. I'll explain it all."

"He needs an ambulance," another man says. I stand back, leaning on my kitchen counter, blood still rushing through my head.

I just beat the shit out of my murdering brother.

He wakes up as they're putting him on a gurney, and Finn comes running inside along with Quinn. His eyes search the room for me, and he immediately comes racing to me, pulling me into his arms.

"Are you okay?"

"Yeah, he's the only one bleeding."

"Fucking bitch!" Kyle yells. "You're going to pay for this. Dearly. I promise you."

"Good-bye, Kyle." I watch as they take him away, and the lead detective asks if he can talk with me for a while, which I agree to. Quinn leaves to go wrap things up at the party.

"Tell me what happened, from the beginning."

"Let's sit in the living room," I reply. Once we're settled, with Finn next to me, I tell him everything, from the day my parents died until today, adding what I know about Kyle following me. "That's it. He admitted that he killed them, and that he tried to kill me."

"We have so many charges here, he'll be put away for a very,

very long time," he replies with a nod. "Here's my card. Call me if you need anything."

He stands and leaves, and Finn follows him out then returns to me. He sits and pulls me against him, not saying anything for a long moment.

"I thought that you'd left me," he admits finally. "I looked around the party for you and couldn't find you. I thought you'd skipped out because you were so angry with me."

"I told Quinn to tell you I was coming here."

"He told me just before I called your phone," he says, and kisses my head. "I don't know that I've ever been that fucking scared in my whole life."

"I wasn't scared," I reply honestly. "Even with the gun, I don't believe he would have hurt me. And I know, that's stupid, because he just admitted to trying to kill me, but I just wasn't afraid of him."

I still don't feel scared. Worn out, and a bit hollow, but not scared.

"I'm just happy you're safe. Let's go back to my place."

"I definitely don't want to stay here," I agree. "I may not be scared of him, but I'll probably never get the image out of my head of him admitting to killing my mom and dad. He smiled, Finn. He thought it was awesome."

"For the money?" he asks.

"Yep. And he was pissed that I lived because I fucked up his plans."

"Son of a bitch. Come on, let me take you home."

"You know, I don't think so." I stand and walk away from him. "I think I really just want to be alone tonight. I'll check into a hotel."

"London, if this is about what happened earlier today—"

"It's not," I interrupt, but then rethink that remark. "Maybe it is, a little. But I want to be alone so I can process everything. Not because I don't love or appreciate you."

"I won't have it," he says, shaking his head. "No. You're coming to my place. I'll give you all the space you want, but you'll be at home with me, not by yourself in a strange place."

"Finn."

He just cocks an eyebrow, and I honestly don't have it in me to fight with him again right now. I'm exhausted, and not a little numb. I don't want to fight. I don't want to prove my point, or dig in my heels.

So I just shrug, grab some sweats, clean underwear, and my clutch, and follow him down to his car, which is miraculously waiting when we get outside.

We're quiet on the short ride to his place. He reaches for my hand, but I pull away and he doesn't try to touch me again. Once inside his condo, I immediately walk into the guest room and shut the door, strip out of the beautiful dress I bought for today, and get into the shower.

Finally, the tears come, hot and hard. My emotions are all jumbled: anger and sadness, disappointment. Fury. Love. Hurt. I can't make sense of any of it as I lean on the shower wall, let the water beat down on me, and give in to the tears as they explode out of me like a burst dam.

When the water starts to turn cold, I get out and dry off, wrap my hair in a towel and my body in a robe, and fall on the bed.

My phone pings with a text from Finn.

> Do you need anything from me, baby?

Tears fill my eyes again. I love him, but I'm so frustrated with him. I take a deep breath and then reply.

> No thank you.

I roll over and turn on the TV, finding some reality TV to play in the background. It dulls the loudness in my head.

I want to forget about all of it, just for a few hours. I don't want to think about Kyle, my parents, or Finn. L.A. Real estate. None of it.

But I do text Sasha because I don't want her to hear about this from anyone else. It would devastate her.

> Hey. Quick FYI, and I'll tell you more later. Kyle showed up at my place, threatened me, and confessed to killing my parents. He's in jail. I'm safe, at Finn's. Gonna sleep now because I'm fucking tired, but didn't want you to hear about it from anyone else.

I reach for a box of tissues and wipe my eyes off, then blow my nose as I wait for Sasha to answer.

Do you need me?

So simple. So Sasha.

Maybe tomorrow?

I smile at her response.

Anytime, love.

Chapter Eighteen

~London~

It was a long night. I slept in fits, and when I woke, I would reach for Finn and then remember everything that happened yesterday. There were so many highs and lows yesterday, I'm not convinced that it wasn't a bad reality TV show.

But it wasn't. It was *my* reality. Everything from the elation of being in love with an incredible man and celebrating his birthday, to being frustrated with that same man, and the horrible scene with Kyle.

I'm sitting on Finn's rooftop, watching the sun come up over the city. I've been up here for about an hour, watching the black sky turn to twilight. Enjoying the quiet. Despite being the city that never sleeps, New York does get quiet in the very early morning hours.

"I made you coffee," Finn murmurs from beside me. I felt him walk up. I glance up at him and see the hesitation in his chocolate eyes as he passes the steaming mug to me and sits next to me on the chaise.

"Thanks," I whisper, and take a sip, then lean my head back as the caffeine immediately hits my system. It's delicious.

He must know that I'm not ready to talk because he wraps his arm around my shoulders, and we sit like this for a while, listening to the city come alive around us. Once my mug is empty, I set it aside, and then lean my head on his shoulder, enjoying the way he feels.

I admit, I missed him last night.

And yet, I'm still so damn mad at him I don't know what to do with myself.

"London," he says softly, and kisses the top of my head. "I would appreciate it if you'd talk to me, sweetheart."

Here we go.

I'm not ready for this conversation, but it looks like we're going to have it whether I want to or not.

I wish he'd just let me go to the hotel last night, just to get a little distance from him to sort everything out.

"London," he tries again.

"I hear you," I murmur, my voice scratchy from a night of crying and nightmares.

"Talk to me," he repeats, and I have to stand and walk to the side of the rooftop, facing away from him as I gather my thoughts. "You know, I can deal with a lot of things, but I absolutely hate the silent treatment."

I turn now, lift my chin, and look him squarely in the eyes.

"I'm not giving you the silent treatment."

"Well, you're not speaking to me, so if that's not the silent treatment, I don't know what is."

I nod and look down at my feet, my arms crossed over my chest, and then back at him.

"Okay, I'm going to be brutally honest. I'm so fucking pissed off."

He frowns. "At me?"

"Hell yes, at you. At pretty much everybody. I told you *last night* what I needed. I explained that I love you, but I really needed a night by myself."

"I didn't want you to be by yourself," he replies, and stands, shoving his hands in his jeans.

"And I can appreciate that. Really. But I'm a grown woman, and I needed a night alone so I could process everything that happened yesterday."

"You had a night alone."

"In *your* house."

"That's right." He steps toward me, but I hold my hand up and he stops. If he touches me right now, I'll walk right into his arms, and I *need* to get my point across. I need him to hear me. "After what had just happened to you, did you seriously expect me to let you go check into a hotel somewhere by yourself?"

"Well, yes, I did."

"Well, fuck that, London. I *love* you. You're my partner. I'm not going to ever do that."

"What you're saying is that you're never going to listen to my needs and give them to me?"

"I'm so fucking tired of fighting with you," he says, and pulls his hand down his face.

"I don't like it either, but you're not hearing me, Finn."

"I'm right here, and I'm listening. Tell me."

I pace away from him in frustration and then turn back to him, willing him to truly hear me this time.

"Most of the decisions in my life haven't been *mine*. The way I eat, how much I exercise, where I live, all dictated to me because of my career. Which I love, and I choose, but it doesn't change that.

"Then we have my brother. Who, by the way, tried to fucking kill me, and I don't think that really set in until about two hours ago, but I digress. Every destructive thing he did in his life? Not my decision. Drugs, homelessness, anger, meanness. All of his shit was out of my control.

"Now I'm in a relationship with a man who is *wonderful*. But he wants to buy real estate and sell my house behind my back. I'm not a weak woman, Finn. I'm actually kind of badass, but it feels like everyone treats me as if I'm made of glass."

"I don't see you as weak," he says, shaking his head. "I just want to take care of you. Is that wrong?"

"Yes, sometimes. I don't need you to take care of me. I can take care of myself just fine, as you saw last night. I need a partner. You called me your partner a minute ago, but this is *not* how you treat your partner. You include her in decisions, and you work together."

"So, locking yourself in my guest room last night was us working through this together?"

Oh my God, I want to strangle him.

"No, this is a valid question, London, because you don't get to have this both ways. We're partners until you decide that we're not?"

"That's not what I did," I reply, but feel a little nudge of guilt because it's kind of what I did. "I just wanted one night to process everything. To think it through. So I could come back to you and we could talk everything out.

"We aren't being productive right now. We're just fighting and hurting each other, and it sucks."

"Okay." He holds his hands up in surrender. "You tell me what you need from me, or need me to do, because I'm not losing you."

"I told you what I needed last night," I say again, and shrug a shoulder, but then decide that if he's going to make decisions without giving me a choice, I'm going to do the same. "And you're going to give it to me."

And with that, I turn and walk back into his condo, collect my bag and shoes, and leave.

As I walk to the front door, he's standing in the living room, his hands still in his pockets, staring at me with a mixture of sadness and frustration.

But I walk out and don't look back, tears already falling down my cheeks.

"The storm is rolling in," I say into the phone. I'm sitting on the sun porch at the house on Martha's Vineyard, watching the clouds rage over the ocean, and I can't help but feel that it's a perfect mirror for the conflict happening inside me.

"Are you okay?" Sasha asks. We've been on the phone for over an hour. I'm in my favorite chair, with a blanket and a box of tissues because I just can't stop crying.

"Do I sound okay?"

"I meant with the storm," she says softly. "I know you hate them."

"I do, but I'm not afraid. The last storm we had when I was here earlier this summer was a shit show. Finn sat with me, and watched the storm with me, and then he made love to me." The tears start flowing again. "Maybe that good memory has replaced all of my fear where it comes to storms."

"Maybe," she says. "So you seriously just walked out on him today?"

"Yeah." I dab at my eyes with a tissue. "I just wanted to be alone, and he wasn't having it. He's not the boss of me, Sasha."

"Right." She clears her throat, the way she does when she doesn't agree with me.

"Say it."

"Well, he's not the boss of you, that I agree with. I mean, even when you're in a relationship, you're still *you*. But he loves you, London, and he was probably super worried about you. I have to say, I wouldn't have been comfortable with you going to a hotel either."

"It's not like I was going to hurt myself."

"Of course not. But you had just been through something

traumatic, and as someone who loves you, I would want to make sure I was nearby in case you needed anything."

"I'm not sick either. I'm just so angry. And I'm sad. Why am I so sad about Kyle? I should hate him."

"He's your brother."

"I mean, I knew that he was a jerk. I didn't know he was clean, and let me tell you, that was a blow."

"Yeah, that's just weird."

"Well, he clearly has mental health issues," I reply with a sniff. "And I am *so fucking pissed* at him for killing my mama and dad. Sasha, he killed them."

"I know, sweetie."

"I keep saying it to myself, but I don't know if I believe it yet. He's a class-A jerk, but I never would have thought that he'd hurt any of us. Not like that."

"You're grieving for all of them," she says, and I nod, even though she can't see me.

"It's not fair. They didn't do anything wrong. I didn't do anything wrong." I can't stop the tears now, and they're flowing freely. I'm a snotty mess. "And now, I have to deal with the fact that my brother, who I've never been particularly close to anyway, is permanently out of my life too, as if he died with them."

"Did you think that you might eventually have a relationship with him?"

"I guess part of me hoped so." I blow my nose and then toss the wet tissue aside for a clean one. "Especially when he told me that he was going to rehab. I *really* wanted it to be true."

"I know."

"And, when he had that gun pointed at me, and said he was going to kill me—"

"Wait, there was a gun?"

"Yeah, and I didn't believe him. I would have just walked up to him and plucked the gun out of his fingers because I *knew* in my heart that he wouldn't hurt me."

"London," Sasha says. "He would have. He did."

"I know. What's wrong with me?"

"Nothing at all. He's your brother and you love him."

"No, not anymore." *Why can't I stop crying?*

"And you hoped that things were different. Not to mention, it was a complete and utter shock that he confessed to killing your parents."

"That's the understatement of the year." I take a deep breath and let it out, watching the lightning fill the sky and illuminate the churning water. "But he did. And I feel like I'm just grieving them all over again, except this time I can walk while I do it."

"You don't have the distraction of an injured leg," she says. "You have to feel the emotions now."

"Well, I don't like it." I swallow hard. "And it didn't help that Finn and I had a big argument before his birthday party and really hadn't resolved that yet."

"What was it about?"

I explain the real estate situation, and Finn asking me to move in with him.

"He doesn't listen to me."

"Hold up." I can hear rustling on the other end of the line, like she's sitting up. "You're pissed because he wants to make sure you're comfortable in L.A.?"

"No, I'm pissed because he didn't *talk to me* about it."

"He doesn't have to ask your permission to buy a house, London."

"No, but he wants *me* to live in it." I frown. "So you're saying I'm wrong about this too?"

"Well, I think he needs to hone his communication skills, and definitely include you in big decisions, but you also could use some polishing on your communication skills. You need to take a step back and look at it from his point of view. At the end of the day, the man just wants to love you."

"He wants to take care of me, and I don't need that."

"He wants to love you," she repeats. "And I know I'm no expert in the relationship game, but I think that part of loving someone *is* taking care of them when they're sad or scared or grieving. You're my best friend in the whole world, and if you want me to kill him and hide the body I'll totally do it, but, London, I think you were being a little extra sensitive yesterday. And I also think, while we're at it, that you're taking a lot of your anger at Kyle out on Finn."

"Maybe," I admit with a sigh, and wipe my eyes for the five-hundredth time. "It just rubbed me wrong, you know? He handed me three properties to choose from."

"So, he didn't say, *Hey baby, let's go find a house together.*"

"No. He'd already been hunting, found three he liked, *furnished*, and told me to pick one."

"Okay, that's a bit much," she agrees. "There's gotta be a happy medium."

"Exactly," I reply, and then feel an ache over my heart. "I hurt him. I hate that I hurt him."

"One of the best things about life is being able to say you're sorry," she says. "I don't think anything has happened here that you can't work out."

"I hope you're right."

Chapter Nineteen

~Finn~

I'm going to spank her ass. Then I'm going to kiss the ever-loving hell out of her.

And then I might spank her ass again.

I'm jogging along the beach, needing to expel some of this frustration before I see her. I just got to the beach house, after the longest night of my life.

Just as I come around the bend toward our houses, I see London standing on the shoreline, her arms crossed over her chest, her white pants and shirt blowing in the wind around her.

Her dark hair is pulled up in a knot at the top of her head. She's not wearing sunglasses.

And I can't wait to have her in my arms.

I jog to a stop about ten feet from her, and before I can say her name, she turns to look at me. Her eyes are full of sadness and pain, and it about brings me to my knees.

But before I can say anything, she walks confidently to me, cups my face in her small hands, and rises up on her toes to kiss me squarely on the lips. Not a quick kiss, but one that sinks in and makes your toes curl.

The kind of kiss that says, *Thank God you're here.*

She pulls back and offers me a small smile. "Hi."

"I'm going to take that kiss to mean that you're not trying to dump me."

She frowns and steps into my arms, hugging me tightly around my torso, her cheek pressed to my chest, and just like that the knot that's been lodged in my throat since she walked out of my condo yesterday morning starts to loosen.

"Let's go inside," she says, taking my hand and leading me into her house. She walks past the kitchen to the living room, and sits next to me on the couch. "I was never trying to dump you."

I brush my thumb over the skin under her eyes. "You're bruised here, London."

"I've been crying a lot," she confesses, and tears fill her eyes again. "My emotions have been all jumbled up for the past few days. And I have to tell you, despite being the one to walk away yesterday, I'm *so glad* that you're here."

"Really?" I tilt my head, watching her. "I tried to get here last night, but that storm blew in and I couldn't reach you. You'll never know how hopeless and frustrating that felt."

I'll leave out the part where I almost decked a flight attendant because he wouldn't let me get on the last plane that *did* land here last night.

"I'm sorry," she whispers.

"Were you okay? Last night?"

She nods. "I was talking to Sasha for a while, and I was thinking about you. That helped."

"I need you to talk to me, sweetheart. I tried this yesterday, and you obviously weren't ready. But I can't do this. I can't be shut out like this, I'm telling you this now."

"You're right," she says. "I was wrong to ask you to leave me be during a traumatic time. Honestly, if the tables were turned, I wouldn't have left you either."

"Wow, you did a lot of thinking last night."

She nods. "I did. And I'm sorry for not communicating with you well. I think we both have room for improvement in that area."

"Agreed."

"The house in L.A. set off my temper, Finn, and I just can't apologize for that."

"Okay, please try to explain to me again *why*. I'm not trying to control you with it, I'm just trying to help."

"I see that," she says. "But you didn't ask me to go house hunting with you. You did it without me and then said, *This is what we're going to do.* I would have been much more receptive had you made the suggestion, and included me in the search."

"Oh." I rub my fingers over my lips, remembering Quinn and Carter warning me that this would be the case, and feel like an ass. "I got so swept up in making it happen for you, it didn't occur to me that you'd want to make it happen with me."

"Yes, exactly," she says with a smile. "If we're going to do this together, we need to truly do it *together*."

"Understood. We'll scrap it for now, and we can revisit it when you're ready."

"Really?"

"Of course." I tuck a stray piece of hair behind her ear. "London, I love you. I want you to feel comfortable, and I do want you to be a part of making decisions. I just truly thought I was taking something off of your plate. I didn't realize that I was adding stress rather than relieving it."

"Thank you." She climbs into my lap and kisses me softly. "Maybe after I get out there for work, you can come join me and we can meet with a Realtor."

"That would be good."

"Okay." She brushes her fingers through my hair, and I want to lay her back and strip her naked, but we're not quite there yet.

Soon, but not yet.

"We need to talk about my brother," she says, and closes her eyes.

"We can talk about anything you like, love."

"I heard from the detective this morning." She opens her eyes and the hurt is back. I absolutely hate that that slimy bastard has done this to her. "He's denying that he said anything about killing our parents, and that I invited him to come to my condo."

"Little cocksucker," I mutter.

"The doorman confirmed that I didn't know he was there, so the breaking and entering is sticking, and he had the gun, so they're charging him with assault."

"Tell me he's still in jail."

"He is, but he'll have a lighter bail, and might be able to post it."

"I'll make a call today. I have friends in criminal law. We'll have the charges stick, and, London, if he does get out, I'll have him followed constantly. He'll never be able to get near you again."

"He doesn't know where I am right now," she says, and then shakes her head. "It's still absolutely ridiculous to me. I mean, I *know* what happened. I was there. But it's almost like it was a movie."

"I wish it was."

"Me too." She lays her head on my shoulder. "I'm so tired."

"Let's go take a nap." I stand with her in my arms and climb the stairs to her bedroom. The covers are still peeled back from her tossing and turning in them all night. I lower her to the floor, pull her baggy shirt over her head, and let it fall to the ground, pleased to find that she's not wearing a bra.

I place a kiss on her collarbone and tug her pants down her legs, along with her panties. She leans on my shoulder as she steps out of them, and rather than lie on the bed, she fists my shirt and pulls it up at the sides, silently telling me that she wants me naked too.

I'm more than happy to oblige her.

I shuck out of my shorts, guide her back onto the bed, and kiss her until neither of us can breathe.

"Missed you," she whispers. "Two days feels like two months."

"Mm," I murmur, agreeing. I can't stop kissing her soft skin. Her shoulder, down to her puckered nipple, and then down her belly. I circle my nose in her navel and then bite the soft skin above her hipbone. "Do you know what I'm going to do to you?"

"I have a pretty good idea," she says with a smile.

"I'm going to spank this perky little ass of yours."

Her head comes off the pillow and she stares at me in surprise. "What?"

"You heard me." But I'm in no hurry. I pull my middle finger through the crease of the back of her knee and smile when she wiggles from being tickled. "I'm going to explore every delectable inch of you. And before I'm done, I'm going to slap your bottom."

"Okay." She smiles and then bites her lip when I gently graze over her pussy lips with my fingertip. "Oh God, Finn."

"You like that?" She nods emphatically, so I do it again and watch her moan. She's always been so responsive. "Nothing turns me on more than turning *you* on."

"Yeah, well, you're good at it," she says, her breath coming faster now. "Sometimes all you have to do is look at me in a certain way, and my panties get wet."

"Is that so?"

"Oh yeah. And when your lips twitch because I'm silly? I just want to jump you."

"Well, jump away, sweetheart."

I kiss her hip and she digs her fingers into my hair, holding on tightly, redirecting me to her pussy, but I shake my head.

"We're doing this my way."

"Why?"

I look up at her until she meets my eyes with hers.

"Because I said so."

"You know, the bedroom is really the only place that I'll put up with that."

I laugh and bite her thigh. Hard. "Oh, don't I know it."

Rather than give her what she wants, I kiss down her legs and tickle her inner ankles with my nose. Her legs are scissoring, her head thrashing back and forth as I nibble and kiss my way back up the other leg, but rather than plant my face between her legs, I flip her over and pull her hips up, then plant my palm on her ass with a resounding *smack*.

"Fuck," she says.

"Did I hurt you?"

She smiles back at me. "Only in a good way."

I slap her once again, and then do exactly what I know she wants the most. I spread her cheeks and bury my face in her folds, licking and sucking. I push my finger inside her and grin when her most intimate muscles clench around it, almost to the point of spasms.

I push her back down on the bed, press her legs together,

straddle her, and push inside her, groaning at the tightness that grips around my cock like a damn vise.

"Jesus, London, you feel damn good."

"Don't stop," she replies. She can't move much in this position, but her hands are fisted in the linens, holding on tightly as I hold on to her ass and thrust in and out, picking up the pace until I feel the orgasm begin to build in the small of my back.

I want to see her beautiful face when I come inside her.

I pull out and flip her back over, spread her legs wide, and slide back home, making us both sigh in absolute pleasure.

"Let my legs go, please."

I comply and she wraps them around my waist, then crooks her finger, asking me to come closer to her.

I lean on my elbows, my fingers buried in her hair, and kiss her firmly, letting my lips roam over her mouth. I bite her lip gently. She arches her neck up as the contractions in her womb begin.

"Finn."

"That's right, baby. I'm right here." I move faster, just a little harder, and watch the flush make its way up her chest and neck and over her face. "Come for me, London."

"Oh my God."

"Come right now."

And she does, coming apart in my arms. I can't hold on any longer, and join her, then hold her close to me, not ready to let go.

"I hated sleeping without you," she admits softly. "I was wrong to leave, Finn."

"We agree on that." I kiss her forehead. "We won't handle things like that again."

"No." Her hand trails down my back to my ass, where she grips on tightly. "Have I told you that I'm rather fond of your ass?"

"Maybe once or twice."

"Well, I am." She kisses my shoulder. "I love you."

"I love you too."

"Do you love me enough to make me breakfast?"

I smile down at her. "Yes, but I don't think either of our places is stocked."

"Right." She scrunches up her nose. "I guess we'll have to go out for breakfast, then."

"You must have worked up an appetite."

"You spanking my ass always makes me hungry."

Chapter Twenty

~London~

Two weeks later . . .

*F*inn should be home any minute. This might have been the longest workday on record, if the amount of missing him I've done is any indication. I leave early tomorrow morning for L.A. to get started on filming, and Finn had to be in court today, so it wasn't possible for him to stay home.

Not to mention I had meetings all day with Fiona and our attorneys, getting contracts under way so I can back her show, and we can get it set into motion.

This show is going to change lives.

But I haven't seen him all day. Which I guess is fine. I mean, I'm going to see him in three days, and then he'll be in L.A. with me for a whole week. I'll be so busy with rehearsals and filming, I'll hardly have time to miss him.

But it's not lost on me that I'm all moved in to his beautiful condo, just in time to pack up to leave.

I have to keep reminding myself that it's only temporary.

I'm standing in the middle of my massive new closet, my hair wet from the shower, trying to decide what to pack and what to wear.

"Do you like your new closet?" Finn asks from the doorway behind me, startling me.

"I didn't hear you." He's leaning there, just watching me, rubbing his forefinger over his lower lip. I want to bite him there. "I'm glad you're home."

"Me too." His lips twitch as he pushes away from the doorframe and walks slowly to me. "I see you got everything unpacked in here today."

"I did. And now I have to pack up to leave tomorrow. Also, have I thanked you for remodeling this for me?"

"About a thousand times." He smiles and kisses my forehead. I just look around at the space. It's massive. Floor-to-ceiling shelves line two walls for shoes and bags. There is a tall dresser on either end, and so many racks for clothes I almost didn't have enough to fill them.

Almost.

"I spoke with the Realtor in L.A. this afternoon. She's lined up five houses for us to see on Sunday."

"That's a lot of houses."

"I want you to have plenty to choose from," he says, his eyes perfectly serious. Since the argument on his birthday, we've both made an effort to listen to the other and communicate our needs clearly.

So far, we're doing well.

"And there's no pressure, London. If we don't see one that you love, we'll keep looking. There's no rush."

"Sounds good. And what do we have on deck for tonight? You were awfully vague on the phone earlier."

He smiles and twists a piece of my hair in his finger, then tips my face up so he can plant the kind of kiss on me that makes the gods weep.

"We'll be spending the evening up on the roof."

"What's up there?"

"Dinner. Relaxation. You and me."

"Well, that sounds just about perfect."

He nods, and then seems to make some kind of decision, because he suddenly lifts me into his arms and carries me to his bedroom.

"I'm not dressed."

"I noticed."

"My hair is wet."

"Sexy as fuck when it's wet," he replies, and tosses me unceremoniously onto the massive bed. My towel opens, falling to either side of me.

"Oops, there went my towel."

"Pity," he says, making a *tsk tsk* sound, and then climbs up onto the bed with me, his hand gliding over my skin and setting me on fire.

Which is what happens *every* time he touches me.

"Do we have time for this?"

"Baby, we can do whatever we want tonight."

"Well then, carry on."

He smirks and watches in fascination as he brushes his finger over my nipple, making it pucker for him. "So responsive."

"That's just anatomy, Finn. You touch it and it puckers."

"Is that so?"

I nod.

"What about this?" He drags his fingertips down my side, and my skin breaks out in goose bumps. "Is this anatomy too?"

"I would think so."

"Hmm." His hand continues down my hip and over my thigh, then up to the crease where my leg meets my torso. "What if I drag my finger here?"

"Feels amazing."

"Anatomy?"

"Maybe."

He narrows his eyes on me and finally, *finally*, pushes that talented finger inside me, and makes a "come here" motion, sending me right off the bed.

"Anatomy, sweetheart?"

"That's you," I gasp. "Jesus, you find my sweet spot fast."

He smiles happily. "That's my job." He pulls my knees up and tucks them against my chest. "Wrap your arms around your legs and hold on."

I do as he asks, hugging my legs against my chest, wondering what he's up to. He hasn't done this before.

Although, Finn's excellent at suggesting new things.

Suddenly he's down on his chest, and his mouth is pressed to my clit. I let my legs fall to the side, but he stops and shakes his head at me. "No, you have to hold them."

"I can't hold on to *anything*."

"Then I guess this stops," he says with a shrug, as if to say, *Too bad.*

I glare at him and pull my legs back to my chest, and Finn just laughs.

"You do know I love you, right?"

"I think so."

He cocks a brow and slides another finger inside me, but I want his mouth back. There's nothing in the world like having Finn's lips wrapped around my clit.

"You're not sure?"

"Well, you stopped what you were doing, and would someone who loves me do that?"

"I see." He nods and presses his lips to me once again, and I have to practically dig my fingernails into my skin to keep from letting go.

It's no use. When I get close to coming, I let go and he stops again, making me groan in disappointment.

"I warned you."

"Your turn," I counter, and push up off the bed onto my knees. "Lie down, Counselor."

He smiles and immediately complies, his dick hard and pushing against the zipper of his slacks. "Yes, ma'am."

"Oh, I get to unwrap you like a present."

"This present is all yours."

"Hell yes, it is."

Rather than start down at his pants, I set to work loosening his tie, pulling it off, and unbuttoning his shirt. I love the way Finn looks in his formal work attire. Especially on court days.

He's fucking hot.

Once his shirt is open, I set to work kissing him, leaving wet spots all over as I move down his torso to his navel and bite him, just to the left of it.

"Ouch."

"I didn't hurt you. Much." I smile up at him, laughing when I see that he's crossed his arms behind his head and he's comfortable, watching me do my thing. "Do you need popcorn?"

"Maybe later."

I chuckle and continue on my journey, exploring the muscular abs, the smooth sides, the little scar over one rib.

"How did you get this?"

"I fell off of my bike when I was nine."

"Ouch." I kiss it. I'm rubbing my body over his, enjoying the way his hard dick feels against my stomach.

"You know you're killing me, right?"

"Who, me?"

"There's no one else here, baby."

"I don't know what you mean."

But I work my way lower, and slowly unfasten his belt, then his pants, and pull them down over his hips and legs, tossing them over the side of the bed.

"How is your skin always tan?"

"I'm Italian," he says. "Permatan."

"Must be nice." My hands glide up and down his legs. I love the way the hair feels on my palms. "I like your legs."

"So you're with me for my legs and my ass?"

"And maybe your tan," I say, and stick my tongue out at him. "And possibly because I love you."

"Possibly?"

"Probably."

He switches our positions again, tucking me under him, bracing himself over me on his elbow. He presses his lips to my cheek. "Just probably?"

I shrug a shoulder, and he grins against my skin, his free hand gliding down my stomach until his fingers press against my clit. "What about now?"

"Yes, it's probable that I love you."

He shifts his hips between my legs and pushes his cock inside me, balls-deep, and cups my face in his big hands.

"London."

"Yeah."

His thumbs are making circles on the apples of my cheeks and he's staring deeply into my eyes.

"I love you, more than I ever thought it was possible to love another person. It seems that you came crashing into my life in one big, magical storm, and I can't remember what it was like before you."

I shift, clenching down on him. "I love you too. So much that it sometimes scares me."

"Baby." He kisses my cheek. "There's nothing to be afraid of."

"There's *everything* to be afraid of." I swallow hard and feel tears threaten as he rears his hips back and begins to move gently. "But I'm so in love with you, and I just don't know what I would do without you in my life."

"You don't ever have to find out," he promises. He's moving in earnest now, pushing us both to the edge of reason, threatening to throw us both off of the edge into oblivion.

He pushes one hand under me, cups my ass, and tilts my hips up, taking the angle to an all-new point of delirium, and I know I'm so damn close.

"Do it," he whispers. "Go over, my love. I'll catch you."

And that's all it takes for me to see nothing but stars explode around me. I'm shivering, breathing hard when I feel him lose it, and I cradle him to me, combing my fingers through his hair.

"I ruined your shower," he says once we've caught our breath. He stands, and holds his hand out for mine. "Come on."

I happily follow him into the bathroom, where he starts the hot water and leads me inside.

I expect him to boost me up against the wall and take me on ride number two, but he doesn't. He smiles softly, contentedly, and soaps up a sponge to wash me with. He's thorough, washing places that didn't even get dirty.

And when he's done, I take the sponge from him and return the favor, washing him down.

I work shampoo through his hair too, trying to ignore his hands gripping on to my ass as I concentrate on the task at hand.

"You're good at that," he murmurs.

"I've been washing my hair for a long time."

"You're also a smartass."

"Oh yeah. I'm a big ol' smartass." He slaps my behind, making me jump in surprise, and then laugh. "You have a thing for smacking my ass."

"I won't deny it."

Once he's rinsed, he dries us both, and then leads me back to the bed, tucking us both under the covers.

"I thought we were going on the roof?"

"We will, in just a minute. I know we'll only be apart for a couple of days, but I want to hold you for a minute longer."

I smile and settle against him, enjoying the sound of his breathing and the quiet. He takes my left hand in his and kisses my knuckles, then each of the fingers, pausing on my ring finger. He's quiet, frowning.

"What is it?" I ask. He's been in such an odd mood today.

"So, when do I get to put a ring on this finger?"

About the Author

New York Times and USA Today bestselling author **Kristen Proby** is the author of the bestselling With Me In Seattle, The Boudreaux, and Love Under the Big Sky series. Kristen lives in Montana, where she enjoys coffee, chocolate, and sunshine. And naps.

BOOKS BY KRISTEN PROBY

ALL THE WAY
Romancing Manhattan

In *New York Times* and *USA Today* bestselling author Kristen Proby's brand new Romancing Manhattan series, three brothers get more than they bargain for as they practice law, balance life, and navigate love in and around New York City.

LISTEN TO ME
A Fusion Novel; Book One

Seduction is quickly becoming the hottest new restaurant in Portland, and Addison Wade is proud to claim her share of the credit. But when former rock star Jake Keller swaggers through the doors to apply for the weekend gig, she knows she's in trouble. He's all bad boy. . . exactly her type and exactly what she doesn't need.

CLOSE TO YOU
A Fusion Novel; Book Two

Since the day she met Landon Palazzo, Camilla LaRue, part owner of the wildly popular restaurant Seduction, has been head-over-heels in love. And when Landon joined the Navy right after high school, Cami thought her heart would never recover. But it did, and all these years later, she's managed to not only survive, but thrive. But now, Landon is back and he looks better than ever.

BLUSH FOR ME
A Fusion Novel; Book Three

When Kat, the fearless, no-nonsense bar manager of Seduction, and Mac, a successful but stubborn business owner, find themselves unable to play nice or even keep their hands off each other, it'll take some fine wine and even hotter chemistry for them to admit they just might be falling in love.

THE BEAUTY OF US
A Fusion Novel; Book Four

Riley Gibson is over the moon at the prospect of having her restaurant, Seduction, on the Best Bites TV network. This could be the big break she's been waiting for. But the idea of having an in-house show on a regular basis is a whole other matter. Riley knows it's an opportunity she can't afford to pass on. And when she meets Trevor Cooper, the show's executive producer, she's stunned by their intense chemistry.

SAVOR YOU
A Fusion Novel; Book Five

Cooking isn't what Mia Palazzo does, it's who she is. Food is her passion... her pride... her true love. She's built a stellar menu for her restaurant, Seduction. Now, after being open for only a few short years, Mia's restaurant is being featured on Best Bites TV. Then Camden Sawyer, the biggest mistake of her life, walks into her kitchen... As Mia and Camden face off, neither realizes how high the stakes are as their reputations are put on the line and their hearts are put to the ultimate test.